A WALKING TARGET

A fist rattled across the door and Ray spun around.

"Who's there?"

"Perry. Open up."

He crossed to the door and drew it back. The sheriff entered without looking up, went to a chair, and dropped down. He bent a long, critical look upon Ray.

"Dog-gone you, anyway," he growled. "Who'd you think that was out there north of town?"

Ray's face brightened. He almost smiled. "Was that you? It sounded like a posse."

"It was a posse, damn it, and I was leading it. We were looking for you."

"I haven't done anything."

"Yet," the sheriff said bitterly. "I wasn't after you, Ray. I was simply trying to prevent you from being put on ice."

"Oh…?"

"Word came this afternoon that Salter knew you were back and had put a thousand dollars on your head…dead."

Gunman

Lauran Paine

LEISURE BOOKS NEW YORK CITY

A LEISURE BOOK®

April 2009

Published by special arrangement with Golden West Literary Agency.

Dorchester Publishing Co., Inc.
200 Madison Avenue
New York, NY 10016

ISBN 10: 0-8439-6150-3
ISBN 13: 978-0-8439-6150-8
E-ISBN: 1-4285-0655-1

Visit us on the web at www.dorchesterpub.com.

GUNMAN

TABLE OF CONTENTS

War at Broken Bow

Chapter One

Buck Carrel looked down over the sweep of his land. There were half-wild whiteface cows, with impatiently bunting calves, wandering over the rich, wiry grassland. It was a good sight and Carrel had fought his way up to it for almost twenty years. It was a solace, a salve for the years gone by working for the big outfits, and a reward for any born and bred cowman. He smiled to himself and built a cigarette while the chunky bay horse stood head down, drowsing. A big, ragged old juniper tree whispered as a little lost zephyr searched through its tough old limbs. The Broken Bow Ranch was owned and operated by Carrel, graying a little over the ears, hard as flint and steady-eyed—as good a cowboy as ever forked another man's string. Now he rode his own horses, for himself, watching over his own little herd and, best of all, on his own ranch. The cigarette tasted better than he could remember ever having one taste before.

Back at the squatty, crudely chinked log barn made of selected and peeled lodgepoles, Buck stalled the bay horse, forked some feed to him, and tossed a great wad of the fragrant timothy over the pole corral fence to four other horses that were nickering impatiently. He scooped up a bucket of water from the creek as he stomped into the log house he had built. It didn't take long to kick up the charred ends of the mesquite roots in the fireplace of field-stone, and encourage a blaze with some dry wood.

The wind was howling when he stretched out on the rawhide couch he had made. It had come up slowly, surreptitiously, sneaking in under the low overhang of the cabin, prying at the shake roof, and then it had capriciously swooped away and tore down over the land with a malicious howl of unfettered glee. Buck lit an old pipe and stretched out in the firelight, the warmth of the fire and the chili beans he had eaten for dinner slackening every muscle and sinew in his body. The wind growled and laughed at him and the sigh of the old junipers standing off another onslaught with swaying grace and indifference made him drowsy. Buck Carrel was at peace with the world. He had what he wanted out of life—peace, his own spread, and his freedom.

A dull, unmistakable crash against the thick, hand-hewn cabin door almost startled Buck out of his wits. He put down the cold pipe, sat up warily, and listened. Only the wind shrieking in the eerie darkness. Slowly he put his feet to the floor, reached out, and slipped the worn old .45 out of its holster draped over the back of a chair, eased himself to his feet, and tiptoed forward. The yellowish light of the lantern flickered when he blew down the mantle. He blew again and the little flame died abruptly.

Standing in the total darkness, the wind sounded malevolent, not as free and friendly as it had when the cabin had been an island of light in the shrouded mystery of the night. He went forward again, listened at the door, heard nothing, and lifted the bar down with silent care. He eased the door open a little, looked out, and swore in surprise. Still holding the door with one hand, Buck pulled it farther open and a savage finger of cold tore into the room. He looked dartingly around, stuck the .45 in the waistband of his Levi's, and grabbed something warm and soft, and tugged.

Buck hesitated to light the lamp again, so he barred the door and dragged his burden over to the old couch and boosted it onto the soft Navajo rugs that covered the rawhide strips. He sat down heavily and mopped his forehead with a dark blue bandanna.

The wind was still trying to find a way into the cabin sometime later when Buck risked lighting the lantern. He sat for another half an hour in the shadows, his gun cocked and ready, but nothing came to make the most of his fears except the wailing, crying volume of the bitter night. He went over and looked at the still figure on the couch and gasped. It was a girl—a bedraggled, wind-blown, completely unconscious girl.

Moving like a man in a trance, slowly and methodically, Buck kicked the fire into life again, tossed some more wood on it, then turned back to the unevenly breathing girl on the couch. He reluctantly admitted that she was pretty, even after the wind had worked her over. Her hair was jet black to match the long, gracefully upcurving eyelashes and the delicate, arched eyebrows. Her flesh was golden tan and firm and her mouth was full with a generous underlip below a small, pert little nose that had a rash of small individual freckles across the saddle. He shook his head dazedly, went over to the lean-to kitchen, and stirred up the fire in the cook stove beneath the big porcelain coffee pot.

The last time a girl had visited the Broken Bow had been two months earlier when his sister and her husband, Black Jack Carlyle, the marshal of Colfax, had driven out in their new underslung carriage. The smell of coffee filled the warm little rooms and Buck methodically poured two cups, carried them in by the couch, and pulled up a chair with a perplexed frown wrinkling his broad forehead.

"Uh . . . sit up, lady, here's some coffee." There was no movement and the frown deepened. "Say, ma'am, I made you some coffee." The eyelashes quivered and Buck's frown disappeared. A look of mild annoyance flashed over his face and he persisted. "Look, ma'am, ya can't sleep here forever. Sit up an' drink a little coffee. It's good for ya."

The long, graceful eyelashes swung upward and a pair of deep purple eyes stared at Buck with an unblinking glance that brought a quick mantle of blood to his face. "Coffee, ma'am?"

The girl's large eyes gradually focused into a look of sardonic amusement. She pushed herself up with an effort, and swept the wealth of black hair behind her with a weak motion. "How did you know I wasn't dying?"

"Well, I didn't exactly."

"Is coffee the only medicine you know of?"

Buck's face dropped to the cup in his hand. He looked like a very small boy caught with a snake in his hand. The girl smiled understandingly, and reached out impulsively, and took the cup. "I'm sorry. I didn't mean it the way it sounded."

"How come you came to the Broken Bow?"

"Broken Bow?"

"Yeah, that's my ranch. I mean, this here is my ranch, the Broken Bow."

"Clever name. What's it mean?"

"The Broken Bow's my brand. Made it up after I found an old Apache war bow broken in two down where I built the barn." The wind crashed into the side of the cabin with stunning force, and the girl winced as it screamed on over the coarse roof. "How'd you happen to come here?"

"I didn't know there was a house here until I opened my eyes and heard you blandly offering me coffee."

"Well, then . . . ?"

"I was riding the stage from Powder River to Colfax." She sipped the hot coffee, and Buck thought of the winding road below his ranch about a mile where the stage rocketed through, twice a day, once in the forenoon, and once late in the afternoon. "We were making good time and I was hoping there'd be no slip up with my stage connections in Colfax, because I want to get home to Dallas, by the First. Anyway, four men suddenly came out of the shadows and shot the lead horse." Her dark blue eyes looked beyond Buck's frown and fear showed in their depths. "We were all ordered out in the wind, the horses were unharnessed and turned loose, and the strongbox was taken. I ran off as soon as I dared." She shrugged. "Between the walk over the dark range in the night and the awful wind I just barely made it up here. Must've fainted in your doorway."

"What happened to the rest of the passengers?"

"There was only one other passenger, a nice-looking young man about your size and build." Her eyes ran approvingly over Buck. "I suppose he's still down there with the coach, or maybe the driver and he started out walking."

Buck downed the rest of his coffee, shrugged into a heavy buckskin coat, and yanked his hat low over his eyes. "Just take it easy, ma'am. I'll be back in a little while." He motioned toward the couch and the fire. "Throw a little wood on the fire if you get cold, an' bed down on the sofa there."

Her oval, golden tan face came up to him. "Where are you going?"

"To Colfax an' start out a search party for the two men, an' also let the marshal know what happened. I'll be back directly."

Her eyes were large and worried when she stood up and watched him go toward the door. "Please. Do you have to go? Won't the passenger and driver get to Colfax safely? I'd rather not be alone for a while."

Buck's slow smile came up. His teeth flashed in the mellow light of the single lantern. "Ma'am, you're safer here than in your own home. Hardly anybody even knows this cabin is here. I only built it last fall. Don't worry." His hand was opening the door and a quick tongue of cold wind whipped past. "I'll be back before you know it." The door slammed behind him and he was gone. The girl looked after him for a help-less moment, then went over and lifted the door bar and dropped it into place. She moved slowly to the lamp, turned it up so high it began to smoke, went over and stirred up the fire, throwing more wood on, then went back and sat on the rawhide couch and pulled a thick, heavy Navajo robe over her legs. The night was cold with a brittle sky where every star was winking down on the subdued range. The girl looked up apprehensively every time the dying wind would throw a gust against the cabin.

Buck had to force the bay horse out of the stall. He pulled back when the wind hit him and humped up ominously when Buck swung aboard. It wasn't far to Colfax—a matter of six miles—but the lessening forces of the wild night made it an uncomfortable journey; the bay horse plodded sulkily along, thinking thoughts about a man who'd ride him out on a night as raw as this one.

Marshal Carlyle was surprised at his brother-in-law at the door. "Come in, Buck. What the devil broke you out of your diggin's tonight? Pardner, I thought sure you, of all people, would be snug as a bug, tonight. What's up?"

Buck smiled at his sister's worried look. "Calm down, Tess. Nothin's wrong on the Broken Bow. It's just that some outlaws held up the stage from Powder River, shot the lead horse, an' turned the others loose after lootin' the thing, then set the driver an' a male passenger afoot." He heaved out of his coat and was careful not to look at his sister as he spoke the next time. "There was a girl passenger, too. She stumbled through the night until she landed at my front door. She's back at the cabin now."

Black Jack Carlyle was a strapping big man with a stubborn, unyielding jaw and a dark complexion that matched his obsidian-colored eyes. He ran an annoyed hand through his hair and looked at his wife. "Wouldn't ya know it? On a night like this. Buck, how about you showin' me where the coach is?"

"Sure." Buck drank the hot coffee his sister brought him, and got up again. "But this here's the sheriff's job, isn't it? You're town marshal, Jack, an' this hold-up happened just below my place on the county road."

Carlyle was tugging at a fleece-lined duck coat. "Yeah. But when Wentworth went over to Gladden, he asked me to sort o' stand by for him until he gets back." He took the big gray hat his wife handed him. "If the damned county'd spend a little money on a deputy, I wouldn't have to do this. Ready?"

Buck blinked owlishly at his sister, and yanked on

his hat and coat. "Say, Tess, did ya ever hear of a woman faintin' from only walkin' a mile or so in the wind?"

Tess Carlyle laughed shortly. "Buck, why don't you get married? Those old cows will never teach you anything about women." She shrugged as her brother moved toward the door. "Besides, your Broken Bow won't ever be a home until there's a woman to put curtains in the windows and cook you something besides chili beans three times a day."

Buck shouldered out of the house behind Jack. He winked solemnly at Tess. "What's wrong with chili beans?"

Chapter Two

Buck waited thoughtfully beside his bay horse until Jack grumpily came riding down the lane from his small barn in back of the house, then he swung up and wordlessly the two men rode through Colfax's deserted, windswept lone street, lined on both sides with wooden stores, weathered and still in the fitful bursts of wind that still tore at the corners of things intermittently.

"She's dyin' down."

The marshal shivered under his big coat. "It's about time. Damn! Don't recollect when I ever saw such a blow in May."

The road was deserted as they rode silently, ploddingly along. The stagecoach was standing awkwardly in the center of the lane, harness sprawled carelessly over the ground; one leather roll-up curtain was flapping forlornly under the final streamers of the windstorm. Carlyle grunted as he led his horse and poked among the effects left behind. "Nothin' here. Buck, how about tracks?"

"Not a chance. The girl said there were four robbers a-horseback, but since this wind's been blowin', they have to have been ridin' two-ton critters to punch tracks in the ground this here wind wouldn't cover up."

"I reckon." Carlyle mounted his horse. "Let's go on up to the Broken Bow an' talk to that there girl."

Buck nodded and led the way over the narrow cow trail that was a short cut to his cabin. "Jack, ever been in Dallas?"

"Once, why?"

"Just wonderin'."

The cabin was dark when they rode up and left their horses in the log barn and walked over to it. "Probably went to sleep an' let the fire burn out." The door opened easily and Buck frowned. "Figgered she'd know enough to bar the door."

The marshal pushed into the room and swore wonderingly. Buck's cabin looked as if a whirlwind had struck it. The furniture was overturned, the lamp was smashed on the puncheon floor, Navajo blankets off the rawhide couch were scattered among the coarser weave Navajo rugs on the floor.

"What in hell!" Jack stood thunderstruck in the middle of the wreckage. Suddenly he started slightly, walked into the kitchen lean-to, fumbled with another lantern, lit it, and brought it back to the combination living and bedroom.

"That there lady you saved must 'a' throwed a fit."

Still dazed as he looked over the wreckage, Buck thumbed his Stetson to the back of his head and frowned. "Well, hell, I don't mind her havin' fits, but, damn it all, she didn't have to tear up my house, too, did she?"

Black Jack burst out laughing. The sight of his brother-in-law shaking his head forlornly over the devastation of his cabin was hilarious—especially Buck's perplexed look. "No, I don't reckon she had to, Buck, but she shore as hell did." The laughter died in his throat and he swooped forward and picked something off the floor. "What's this?" Buck sidled up and looked down on a small white handkerchief with fancy English initials embroidered across one corner.

"Handkerchief with. . . ."

The night was dead still. The last of the wind had scurried south, and clear stars were shimmering over the deathly quiet range when the violent explosion of a .45 roared out of the darkness. Jack staggered under the impact of the slug and sank to the floor. Buck's gun was out and belching before the first echo had died away. The first shot shattered the lamp into a thousand oily fragments; the second shot went blindly out the open door after the orange slab of flame from the ambusher's gun. Buck was on the floor beside his brother-in-law, facing the door.

"Jack? Where'd ya get it?"

Mumbled profanity, brittle with pain, answered him. "In the gizzard, I reckon. Can't feel a damned thing but blood under my hand."

Buck explored the marshal in the darkness. His hand came away from the ribs, sticky and warm. "Side, Jack. Lie still a minute an' I'll set up the sofa." He closed and barred the door, set up the sofa, and tossed a wadding of blankets on it, lifted Jack as gently as he could, and rolled him out full length on the couch. "What in hell d'ya reckon's up, anyway?"

"Buck, I'll lay ya two to one that there mysterious girl o' yours didn't leave your cabin willingly. Fer some danged reason those renegades tracked her over here some way, an' kidnapped her after you left to come to Colfax."

"It's possible but don't make sense, a girl tearin' up my house like that." He cast an apprehensive look around the eerie room, went over and hung a rug over the single window in the front of the house, and rolled a cigarette. "Well, we're bottled up in here till mornin', Jack, so I might as well boil some water an' tie up your gizzard."

Dawn wasn't far off, it turned out. Buck located the ragged wound, cleansed it, and wrapped it securely with a clean feed sack dishtowel. "That'll hold you till you can get to Colfax. Lucky shot, at that. Plowed through a lot of blubber but didn't go on into your innards."

"What d'ya mean, blubber? Why. . . ."

"All you married men got it. It seems like it sort o' goes with gettin' mashed potatoes every day fer dinner. Now, us single men stick to nonfattenin' chili beans an' never dig our graves with our teeth."

Jack felt better, the dull throbbing in his side holding itself to a minimum so long as he remained still. "Yeah," he came back sarcastically. "Chili beans an' old dishtowels fer bandages . . . us married men got bandages around the house, anyway."

"Now you just simmer down, old-timer, an' keep your gun in your hand while I go out and harness up a buggy horse. We'll take you home where Tess can take care of you all nice and proper, an' stuff you with pie an' potatoes."

Jack's profanity followed Buck out of the cabin but died as soon as the door closed. With a grimace of pain the marshal pulled himself to his feet, and, ignoring the cold little beads of sweat that popped out on his forehead, he staggered over to the window, lifted the rug, and rested his six-gun, cocked and ready, in the opening where he could watch Buck catch and harness his driving horse. If the night riders were still about and aimed on getting Buck, Jack grimly promised them six lethal surprises of lead.

With Jack's saddle horse tied to the tailgate, they drove down through the cool dawn toward Colfax. They passed the lonely stage and scowled at it.

"Don't make sense to me, Buck. Holdin' up the stage isn't anythin' out o' the ordinary, but what in hell we got shot at fer, I can't figger out."

Buck started visibly. "You still got that handkerchief?" Jack rummaged in his pants pocket and brought forth a bedraggled little piece of cloth. He looked at it quizzically and handed it to Buck. "It's one o' them things women carry. Y'know, it's for show, not blow."

Buck smoothed it out on his knee and studied the initials. C.J. He frowned and looked at the undulating hips of the horse after giving the handkerchief back to Jack, who studied it gravely, then pocketed it again.

"Might mean somethin' later on, but right now it's no help at all."

Tess met them at the door with a worried, drawn face. She bustled ahead and opened Jack's bed and helped him into it, then turned on her brother with flashing eyes. "Buck Carrel. What do you mean bringing my husband home half killed?"

"I didn't do it, Tess. We...."

"You had no right taking him out in the middle of the night over a silly old stage robbery. His job is here in Colfax, anyway, an', besides, what kind of people do you keep up at the Broken Bow? First it's a fainting woman, then it's killers in the dark. Buck Carrel, you'd better...."

"G'night Jack ... er ... I mean, g'mornin', see ya later. *Adiós* Tess, dear." He darted for the door and Buck wanted to laugh as the slipstream came back to him before the front door slammed. "Pie an' potatoes an' clean bandages an' all that screechin'. T'hell with it. I'll take the chili beans!"

Colfax was coming to life slowly, groggily. Buck rubbed his whisker-stubbled jaw and decided to eat at the Chinaman's. He walked over and entered casually, squatted on the unbending bench in front of the counter, nodded to the slitted, beady black eyes that peeked out at him from a small window in the wall. "Make it two eggs an' coffee, Sam."

The beady eyes disappeared and a sound like a thousand bees, each with his rear end caught in a trap, emerged from the cooking end of the café. The door banged behind him and Buck turned casually and nodded to the big, well-dressed man who plumped down beside him. Colonel Rash was a broad-shouldered, frosty-eyed man in his late fifties; he was the owner of the Northwestern Stage Company.

"Say, Colonel, I don't know whether you know it yet or not, but you got a stage settin' out by my ranch on the road with no horses. Was stuck up last evenin' an' the strongbox was taken off."

Rash swore a violent oath and jumped up. "Are you shore, Buck?"

Buck scratched his forehead solemnly and looked at the big man. "Well, dammit, considerin' that I haven't had any sleep for the last ten hours or so on account of that robbery, I'm about as sure as I can be."

The colonel swung toward the door. "I'll go tell Black Jack. This is another outrage that he'll have to. . . ."

"Hold on a minute, Colonel. Jack's already been slightly shot over the damned robbery, an' he can't do nothin' fer ya until he's back on his feet."

"Good Lord! Sheriff Wentworth's out of town,

too." The big head came around with that peculiarly abstract look on its face that executives get when they're making a quick decision. "Buck, you're the new marshal an' sheriff until one of the elected officers gets back on duty." Buck opened his mouth wider than his eyes. "Don't argue, Buck, as chairman of the board of founders of the town of Colfax, I hereby appoint you *pro tem* marshal."

"What's that, Colonel?"

It was wasted breath; Colonel Rash was gone in a feverish haste, his coattails streaming after him like banners. Buck turned back and regarded the greasy, lead-colored eggs with distaste, and shook his head mildly. "All I came in here for was breakfast."

Before he finished eating, Colonel Rash and two other worried-looking merchants hustled in. The colonel wordlessly pinned a shiny new sheriff's badge on Buck's rumpled shirt, and stepped back with a broad smile.

"That makes it official, Buck. Congratulations." He rubbed his hands together unctuously, and his eyes hardened. "Now then, Sheriff, there was three thousand dollars in that strongbox. Do your duty. If you want me, you'll find me at the stage company's office."

The three men filed out. Buck watched them go, turned back, and looked into the grinning, bland face of Sam the Chinaman. "Sam, how'd ya like to be a deputy sheriff?"

Sam's grin disappeared in a flash. "No thlankeee, please. Sam dlo all time cookkee nlice leggs flor all slame eatee blig bleakfos flor nlew sleriff. Dleputy all time get klill. No bleakfos. Nlo thlankeee."

Buck sighed, paid his bill, and walked out into the sunlight of a warm new day. All he had to do was find

four highwaymen, a mysterious and very beautiful
girl, a strongbox with $3,000 in it—and keep from be-
ing killed while he was nosing around, before he
could go back to the Broken Bow. He shrugged and
took his jaundice-eyed buggy horse down to the livery barn. "Feed him good, Oscar. He might have to
do me for a saddle horse before this day's over."

The liveryman nodded absently, whistled through
his fingers, and turned Buck's horse and buggy over
to the watery-eyed man reeking of whiskey who
came ambling up from the shadowy, cool interior of
the barn. A second look and the liveryman's eyes
widened. "You the sheriff now, Buck?"

"Temporarily, I reckon, why?"

"What a relief. I've been wonderin' what to do
with that there horse. Wentworth's out of town,
an'. . . ."

"What about the horse?" Buck turned and looked
casually at a saddled and bridled bay mare standing
sleepily in a tie stall. The rein ends were dangling
about six inches under the bridle, evidently broken
off short.

"The danged critter was standin' in there when I
come down this mornin', an' Hubert, that's the
hostler, says she come in here all by herself without
no rider about ten or eleven o'clock last night."

"Does Hubert know fer sure when she came in?"

The liveryman shook his head promptly. "No,
Hubert only knows two things, for sure . . . when to
feed the horses, an' when it's safe to drink himself
into a staggering stupor."

Buck walked over and led the mare out to where
he could look her over closely. There was a ragged
piece of cloth in the gullet of the saddle. He removed

it forcibly and palmed it. The bay mare was dog gentle as they walked around her. "Ever see her before, Oscar?"

"Nope. Not only never seen her before, but that there cross dot brand on her right stifle is a new one to me. She's no local animal, I can tell you that for sure."

"Mouth her?"

"Yeah. She's smooth. Her age ain't huntin' her, though. Nice mare, like to get her for any livery string. 'Pears plumb gentle." He picked up a cotton cord, ran it through the rein chain loops, tied a quick knot, twisted a stirrup, and swung aboard. "Nice mare." He swung her down the lane of the barn, rode to the end, turned her, and started back. "Be a good rental critter, Buck. I'd like to. . . ."

It happened so fast Buck hardly saw her fire. One treacherous side whip and Oscar was on his hands and knees looking up stupidly at the calm, indifferent bay mare. "Yeah. Make a fine animal in your livery string. Good fer old women and children. Let's give her to old Doc Evart, the undertaker. He's been complainin' business ain't so hot since the town fathers passed that ordinance forbidding guns in the city limits."

Oscar got up red-faced, threw a venomous glance at the patiently waiting bay mare, and led her back to the tie stall. Buck was already down the plank sidewalk, his spurs ringing musically as he headed toward Colonel Rash's office to talk to the stage driver, when he stopped dead still for a long moment. He sauntered over in front of the general store and began to roll a cigarette with detached casualness. He struck a match, exhaled a mighty cloud of bluish smoke, fished the scrap of cloth out of his shirt pocket that he had pulled from under the seating leather of the saddle, up near the gullet, and stared down at it.

It fitted together pretty well, in a way, but in another way it just didn't figure at all. He pocketed the slip of cloth and continued on down to Rash's office. "Colonel, where's the driver who was on that stage last night?"

The stage line owner smiled and bobbed his head. "You happened along at an opportune moment, Buck . . . er, Sheriff, I meant to say. He's in my office. Come on in. I was just going to talk to him myself."

Chapter Three

The driver was a weathered, wiry man with faded blue eyes and a good-natured, stubborn set to his face. He nodded to the colonel and Buck, but didn't get up. The colonel seated himself behind his highly polished desk with a flourish, motioning Buck to another chair. He was frowning importantly at the driver, who watched them both with alert, bird-like eyes.

Without taking his eyes off the driver, the colonel spoke. "This is one of my oldest drivers, Sheriff. Name of Cash Todd. Now then, Cash, tell us. . . ."

"Let me handle it, Colonel." Rash looked up quickly, a startled, indignant flash in his eyes. Buck rolled another cigarette and tossed the sack to the driver. "Cash, did ya see anythin' before they jumped ya?"

Todd caught the tobacco sack and began to manufacture a cigarette. He struck the match with his left hand and inhaled deeply as he tossed back the sack. Buck pocketed it absently. "No, sir, nary a thing. All of a sudden there they was, four of 'em. Hard-eyed *hombres*, too. All strangers. Took the box, kilt one horse to stop me, an' turned the others loose. Slickest piece of work I ever seen."

"What happened to your passengers?"

Cash snorted in disgust. "They was a gal aboard, ridin' from Powder River. She was to take the mornin' coach outta Colfax, headin' south. Said she was goin' to Dallas. I dunno what happened to her. She must 'a' run off in the night. Scairt, more'n likely. Then there was a young feller who walked on into Colfax with me. I didn't see him after we got here."

"Did he tell you who he was, or where he was goin'?"

"Nope. We talked about the robbery as we was walkin' to town, but that's about all. Never even asked him where he was goin', come to think of it."

Buck ground out his cigarette and got up with a slow smile. "Well, I reckon that's that, Colonel. Thanks, Cash. *Adiós.*"

Buck was in the livery barn, picking up the lines to his horse and sitting in the seat of his buggy when Colonel Rash came trotting up, puffing as if he had run a mile. "Where ya goin', Buck?"

"Back to the ranch."

"But what about the robbery? Ya can't just up an' ride off. . . ."

"Aw, simmer down, Colonel. I got some chores to do, then I'll be right back."

"But every minute counts . . . that money might be going south to the border right now." The pale blue eyes were alternating between a plea and a look of pompous indignation.

Buck nodded thoughtfully. "Yep, it might at that, but I still got a little checkin' aroun' to do at the Broken Bow, an' I'm goin' to do it." He flicked the lines slightly and the horse began to move forward. He tossed a sardonic smile at the open-mouthed man behind him. "If I'm not back in a couple o' hours, bring out a posse, will ya?"

He drove out of town with a sour look on his face.

The day was warm and clear, and, by the time Buck got to where the stage had been, it was gone. Only the dead horse remained, dragged off to the side of the road to ripen and grow mellow while the persistent solicitations of the buzzards and coyotes commemorated the event. Buck looked at the spot with a saturnine frown. He was still trying to fit some loose thoughts into an acceptable pattern when the horse stopped patiently at the little log barn. Buck clambered down stiffly and removed the harness, gave the horse a fond pat on the rump that started him off in search of feed, and pulled the buggy under the shade of the barn overhang.

The house looked even more dismal in the daylight. He swore with feeling and began to set the place to rights. Rancor arose within him as each minute passed, and, having finished arranging the furniture and cleaning up the place, he swore openly and bitterly as he mopped the slippery coal oil off the floor, where a large stain remained, which he wisely covered with a Navajo rug.

Composed again, but still irritated, Buck cooked a large noon meal and sat down at the kitchen table to muse over the sudden tempest he had been so suddenly projected into. He was still smoking and looking drowsily at the blank wall where an assortment of frying pans hung from a deer antler rack, when a movement caught his eye over toward the door. Somewhere a long way off a horse whinnied and was answered. He turned casually and looked toward the clear sunshine that came in through the open door. His eyes widened and the stubby cigarette burned slowly, perilously close to his fingers, unheeded. A big young man was standing in the doorway, broad-shouldered and steel-lipped. He had a gun in his fist that was pointing directly at Buck's recently filled midriff. "Shuck that gun, mister!"

"Dammit all anyway. Now wait a minute. I'm a peaceable man. . . ."

"Shuck it an' shut up!"

Buck sighed in resignation and dropped his gun to the floor beside his chair. "Who in hell are you, anyway? This damned ranch's gettin' plumb crowded with strangers lately."

The man moved into the room, still holding the gun, and kicked the door closed behind him. "Where's that handkerchief?"

"What ya talkin' about?"

There was a quiet moment before the grim-faced man spoke again and Buck unmistakenly heard the snap of his gun hammer. "You know what I'm talkin' about. Where's that damned handkerchief? The one that woman lost in here before she left last night. I seen you an' another *hombre* lookin' at it last night, an' I Want it." The broad shoulders rose and fell. "After I get it, you'll be safe, but until I get it, somebody's liable to get hurt."

Buck nodded gently, his eyes narrowed and hard. "Then it was you that shot in here last night an' made off with that girl?"

"That's right, cowboy. Now, gimme that rag!"

"I don't have it. It's in the marshal's office in Colfax."

For a second, the wide eyes wavered under the thick, bushy black eyebrows, and then the hard, full mouth twisted downward. "You see the initials on it?"

Buck shrugged and lied with aplomb. "Saw some fancy signs on it, but ain't sure what they were."

For a long, silent moment the gunman looked

hard at Buck and shifted his weight on his booted feet. There was a musical tinkle as his spurs rattled in the still room. "All right, pardner, if it's in the marshal's office, I'll get it . . . but you won't be around to know it."

Buck didn't wait for the last word to die out before he went into action. He had anticipated the invader's intentions and made a wild jump for his gun. A thunderous roar filled the room and Buck's right leg went violently sideways as a slug knocked the high heel off his boot. His own gun was in his hand and he rolled as he shot. There was no attempt at accuracy—just a roaring, crashing, deafening exchange of bullets. The stranger backed abruptly away, spun, and made a wild charge for the door. Buck rose up swiftly and let go with his last shot. The door slammed violently under the savage impact of the slug as he got to his feet, awry and disheveled. He swore as he changed into his spare pair of boots.

Buck felt uncomfortable and naked when he slipped outside and furtively fed his horses and dodged back to the house. It was getting dark and he waited patiently for the shadows to become dense enough before risking the ride to Colfax. Feeding the horses was one thing. A bushwhacker wouldn't have too good a chance at getting him then, but riding along the unprotected road was an invitation to murder. He loaded a second six-gun and rammed it into the waistband of his pants, shoved extra cartridges into the empty loops in his belt. He ate a bowl of cold chili beans and paced the cabin in fretful patience. Night came fast. The last of the spring twilight suddenly turned to darkness and a still, hushed foreboding settled over the Broken Bow.

Buck opened the door a crack and let his eyes

become accustomed to the dingy blackness as he studied the range south, toward the county road from his barn. He knew he'd be safe in getting to the barn, saddling up, and riding out of the yard, but beyond that he had misgivings. Whoever the gunman was, and whatever was behind his trigger finger, didn't matter right then. What mattered to Buck were his chances of arriving in Colfax on top of his horse.

He moved stealthily out of the house, and made it safely to the barn. The bay horse snorted softly in the darkness and rolled his eyes. Buck growled at him reassuringly as he dragged the saddle off its rack. Somewhere, outside, a rock rattled on the hard ground. Buck froze for a second, let the saddle drop, drew his gun, and crept to the partly opened door of the barn. Not fifty feet away he saw a phantom-like figure squat quickly out of sight in the tall grass. A saddle horse was standing a little way off, looking puzzled. Buck upped his gun, cocked it, and rested it against the doorjamb.

"You, there in the grass . . . come up out of there with your hands high!"

A frightened figure came up slowly and a nasal, reedy voice spoke garrulously in the darkness. "What in hell's goin' on aroun' here?"

Buck let the air out of his lungs in a long, slow snort. "Colonel Rash. Just what in hell are you doin' slippin' aroun' here in the grass?"

Rash put down his hands and walked over to the barn, shaking his head. "I declare. I just don't know what's goin' on around here, Buck. Dammit all, you said to come up after you if you didn't return to town in an hour or so . . . so I came."

Buck appraised the stage company owner with

quizzical eyes and holstered his gun. "I was just being sarcastic. Go get your horse, an' we'll ride on into town an' bring back a posse. Somethin' damned fishy is goin' on aroun' here."

"Yeah? Like what?"

A flashing figure dashed out of the night, scooped up the reins of Rash's horse, and went plunging out of sight. Buck felt the colonel stiffen beside him. "Like that," he said laconically. He reached out instinctively and yanked Rash inside the barn, a pistol crashed close by, and Buck dropped to the hard ground. Rash, wide-eyed, went down beside him.

"Buck, you hit?"

"No. But if I'd've stayed standin' up, there was a good chance of it."

"Oh, I see. For a minute. . . ." Two snarling roars rocked the night and the bay horse snorted and pawed in terror. Buck turned a cold eye on the man beside him.

"Got a gun?"

"Why, yes, as a matter of fact I have two. One's a six-gun an' the other's a Derringer."

"Well," came the dry reply, "if I was you, Colonel, I'd get ready to use one of them. Somebody don't want us to leave the Broken Bow alive."

He inched forward, shoved the door open a crack, and peered out. The Stygian darkness made visibility very poor. "Don't see anything but. . . ." A tongue of livid flame leaped out at him and a slug slammed into the oak beside his head. Buck wriggled backward with awkward speed. "Damn. I'd like to get one crack at that *hombre*."

He crawled forward again, peered cautiously out, and fired twice. A rifle off to the left answered him. He turned to fire at it and the pistol on his right drove another slug into the quivering door. Buck swore under his breath and sidled back beside the colonel. "Damned if there isn't two of 'em. Hell, I thought my visitor came alone."

"What visitor?"

"Never mind that right now. I'll tell you later, if we live." He pushed himself upright tenderly. "Come on, that door's a dead giveaway. Follow me."

Feeling their way through the darkness, they crept over to the hay room, clambered on top of the stack, and eased carefully out onto a small overhanging roof that lay, like an afterthought, along the barn side of the building. A breath of cool air swept over them as they inched along carefully until they were in a position to command the surrounding countryside.

Buck nudged Rash. "See that clump of scrub oaks over there?" Rash nodded wordlessly. "One of 'em's over there. Draw a bead an', when I say fire, let go. Just shoot once, then drop over the edge of the roof and run like the devil for the house."

Chapter Four

Colonel Rash drew a shiny .45, cocked it methodically, and pushed it out arm's length. Buck hissed, and two belches of fire split the night. Somewhere a hoarse grunt of surprise erupted into profanity. From opposite positions, the attackers fired almost instantly. They kept up a vicious raking of the barn, until the one with the rifle suddenly saw the running silhouette in the darkness and whirled, levering and firing with alacrity. Buck and Rash made it to the cabin with a couple of inches to spare as the last rifle slug ripped a long, snake-like splinter off the log by the door. Rash went over in a blob of groaning profanity as he collided with the couch.

Buck barred the heavy door, sighed with resignation, helped Rash to his feet, and set the couch up for the second time that day with a doleful, uncomprehending wag of his head. "People oughtta live in caves."

"What d'ya mean?"

"Nothin'. Look, Colonel, those fellers have us pretty well holed up. We can't go on like this forever. I'm goin' to slip outside an' try to nail one of 'em. You stay here an' fire every once in a while . . . maybe they'll think we're still in here together." He moved toward the door again and hesitated as he opened it. "I don't suppose you'll know me from the other *hombres*, though, will you?"

"That's no problem, Buck."

"No? Not for you, maybe. . . ."

"Nor you, either. I just won't shoot to kill unless I can see what I'm shootin' at." Buck nodded with a broad smile, and disappeared. Rash barred the door after him and eased back the sole window in front of the square little house, resting his gun on the sill, as Black Jack Carlyle had done the night before.

A pale glimmer of a late moon came up. It was nothing more than a thin sliver in the sky and added practically nothing but a watery sheen to the dark gloominess of the night.

Buck knew his land well. He circled cautiously around the cabin and began a crouching, stealthy hike through the darkness. He figured the pistol gunman was still somewhere near the clump of scrub oaks while the rifleman might be anywhere, but was probably stalking the cabin by now. The little fringe of trees, darker outlines against the ebony shadows, loomed up ahead. He cocked his pistol and went on, wide-eyed in an effort to pierce the gloom. Suddenly he caught sight of a movement up ahead and flattened against the earth. A man was coming toward him. He raised the pistol and waited. There was something vaguely familiar about the walk of the man; he wasn't tall but a peculiar agility sent him bounding along on the balls of his feet.

"Don't you move." The words hissed and the man froze in the darkness. Buck came up to his knees slowly, squinting up at the pale oval of a face.

His effort to pierce the man's identity almost ended fatally. Before he could fire the two remaining slugs in his pistol, the stranger took two quick steps forward, swung his foot savagely, and Buck's wrist sent a jolt of pain up to his shoulder. He came up with an oath and threw himself on the smaller man as the other's gun flashed dully in the darkness. The hot muzzle blast was so close he could feel the sting of the powder and his ears set up a shocked vibratory hum inside his head, but he was on his man. They went down in a flurry of flailing arms and gouging fingers.

The smaller man's strength was surprising and his lithe agility, wiry and frantic, left Buck hitting where he had been as he squirmed away, scooped up his gun, and fired again. This time Buck felt only a tremendous jar and quick, merciful darkness. He sank forward in the rank grass and the shorter man disappeared into the gloom with madly tinkling spurs fading musically as he ran.

Rash had heard the shots. An instinctive inner sense told him that Buck had been discovered. He flung open the door and went out into the night like a wild horse. Just beyond the edge of the cabin he came up face to face with something that, in the split second he observed it, looked like a billowing, round-chested ghost. A shadowy arm arched suddenly and Rash collapsed. The wraith bent over him quickly, turned him over, peered intently into his face, and ran into the cabin, slamming and barring the heavy door with a loud crash. A rifle crashed suddenly not far away and the door quivered under the impact. The wraith backed hurriedly away.

Buck came to with a throbbing splitting headache that sent waves of nausea over him. He sat up weakly and ran a shaking hand over his head. A sticky, ragged gash down the center of his scalp indicated the course of the assailant's slug. He felt around in the grass for his gun, couldn't find it, and swore with feeling as he began a four-footed crawl toward the cabin. Suddenly the night erupted as a gun crashed. Buck heard the bullet smack into his door. He gritted his teeth and pushed forward, convinced that the attackers were smoking Colonel Rash out of the house. Gaining strength as he crawled, he sidled around the edge of the cabin toward the door and fell over a still, warm form. In a moment of surprise and consternation he felt for the downed man's gun, found it, and held it against the man's chest as he peered into the face of Rash.

"Dammit. This don't make sense," he said out loud but under his breath. "If Rash ain't in my riddled cabin, who in hell is?"

He ran an exploring hand over the colonel's body, found only a lump on the head as the still form began to quicken into life again. Buck held Rash down until the colonel's full faculties had returned, then he propped him against the cabin wall and gingerly touched his matted, puffy scalp wound.

"Who's in the house?"

Rash felt of his bruised head and made a wry face. "Damned if I know. I come bustin' aroun' the side of the house an' somethin' long and willowy-looking cracked me over the head."

Buck sighed and carefully wagged his lacerated head in bewilderment.

"Well, sittin' here ain't too healthy."

"No, but at least it's better'n gettin' hit an' shot at every time ya move."

Buck opened his mouth to speak, froze quickly, and laid a restraining hand on the colonel's arm. Two distinct dark objects were moving in on the cabin. Apparently by prearranged signal, the outlaws were converging by individual tangents on the front door. Buck flattened and motioned Rash to do likewise. There was an ominous glint of pale, dark light on a rifle in the hands of one of the attackers and a pistol in the hands of the other, smaller man.

Buck nudged Rash and whispered to him in a menacing voice. "That there short 'un with the pistol's my meat. I owe that *hombre* a scalp treatment."

Rash's whisper came back in consternation. "Where in hell's my pistol?"

"I got it, lost mine. Use that Derringer you said you had." There was a frantic rustling in the grass as Rash dug out the small gun. "They're almost to the door. When they get there, let 'em have it."

"Their backs will be to us. Can't we . . . ?" Rash wondered.

"T'hell with that chivalry stuff. I don't know what it's all about, but I'm not givin' them any more of a break than they'd give me."

Rash shrugged and lapsed into a slit-eyed silence, watching the two men come up. They were up to the door and Buck's gun was cocked and lined up when one of them spoke. "Open it, an' be quick about it."

Buck hesitated, as did Rash, although both their guns were aimed and ready. Again the voice came back to them. "Dave, slip over to that there window an' see if ya can get a bead on one of 'em."

The voice hadn't been lowered and Buck had the uncomfortable feeling that he'd heard that man somewhere before and not too long before, either. He let his gun barrel dip a little as the taller of the men edged up to the window and risked a quick peek inside. A terrific blast shook the ground where Buck and Rash were lying. Both of the outlaws went down to their knees in shock. Buck turned a startled look at Rash. "Damn! That there was my old shotgun.

Whoever shot it pulled both triggers at the same time."

The tall outlaw crawled rapidly toward his smaller companion, his hat gone and his pale face a lot paler. "Gawd"—the voice was husky with fright—"that was close, Cash." The smaller man nodded quickly as his companion got to his legs and crouched. "I had enough. Hell, let 'em keep it. We'll be outen the country, anyway. Come on."

The men both stood up furtively, tossed apprehensive glances at the completely devastated window, and started to slip away. Buck raised his gun again and his cold voice cut through the gloom like the toll of doom. "One more step, *hombres*, an' you're dead men!"

The unnerved renegades froze. Buck nudged the colonel. "Their guns, quick." Rash went forward with his ridiculous little gun jutting out in front of his stomach. He tossed the rifle back toward Buck and stuck the pistol from the smaller man into his waistband before he turned uncertainly toward Buck.

"Tell your pardner in the cabin to come out."

"Our pardner?" The big man's voice was incredulous. "We figgered you fellers was in there." He shook his head emphatically. "Ain't no pardner o' mine. Dang' near blew my head clean off the rest o' me."

Buck flicked his tongue over his lips in puzzlement. "Well, dammit, if it ain't your *compadre* in there, who in hell is it?"

"How should we know? We come up here together. Just the two o' us."

Buck got to his feet, kicked the carbine out of his way, and walked up close. He squinted his eyes at the men and stepped back with a slow nod. "I recognize both o' you now." He turned to Rash. "This here long-legged, bushy-haired, beady-eyed outfit is the *hombre* who damned near salivated me this aft'noon an' . . ."—his gun barrel jutted toward the smaller man—"that there's Cash Todd, in case you don't recognize him. Your best driver."

Colonel Rash, sensing the sarcasm in Buck's voice, gave a small start and stepped in close with an oath to peer into Todd's face. "Good Heavens, Buck, it *is* Todd!" He turned ferociously on the grizzled driver. "Damn you, Cash. I've a notion. . . ."

"Rope it Colonel." Rash shut up and Buck motioned to the taller of the outlaws. "You, mister, turn aroun' an' knock on that there door."

"Look, *hombre*, that bird inside's got a shotgun. I ain't. . . ."

Buck's gun bore down on the man. "Do like I said, hardcase. What's the difference whether you get it through the door or from me? Hit that door!"

The outlaw thumped heavily with his fist.

Buck nodded grimly and raised his voice a little. "Open up in there. The war's over. If you don't open up, I'll blast my way through, usin' these renegades for a shield."

The tense men heard the bar drop before they saw the door swing inward. Buck motioned the men forward and they trooped into the room where the darkness was almost impenetrable. "Colonel, keep a gun on 'em. I'll light a candle." The light was a rich, faltering yellow but it was sufficient. Buck looked up quickly when the taller of the renegades gasped and exploded into a profane tirade.

"Shut up, you." The man subsided slowly, reluctantly. Buck turned to Rash. "Colonel, there's a couple o' lariats hangin' on the wall over there. Get 'em an' tie up these two would-be killers."

His eyes widened as he looked beyond the colonel into a stunning pair of large, horrified eyes that stared out steadily at him from beneath luxurious, upcurving lashes. "You!" The girl didn't move and Buck frowned slightly. "Ma'am, just who the devil are you an' what's this all about?"

The girl's supple body came forward from the shadows with a rhythmic sway. She dropped the shotgun and unconsciously rubbed a sore, outraged shoulder. "I'm his sister." She pointed toward the steely-eyed man. "I tried to talk them out of it."

"Out of what? Please, ma'am, let's start at the beginnin'."

The girl sat down beside Buck on the couch as Rash tugged sadistically at the ropes he was binding the furious outlaws with. "My brother is the tall man over there."

"What's his name?"

"David James. He's. . . ."

An elemental sound that resembled the familiar— "Awk."—erupted from Colonel Rash. "Y'mean this here one with the bushy hair an' straight eyebrows is Dave James? The . . . the cousin o' Jesse?"

She nodded wearily. "Yes. He's my brother. He and the other man planned to rob the stage. I was forced to go along with them so's the robbery wouldn't look suspicious. After they took the box and turned the horses loose, they were to give me a horse and let me go on home, to Dallas." She frowned slightly at an unpleasant recollection. "The horse bucked me off and I found this cabin before I fainted. I really wasn't hurt, though, just upset about the robbery and being afoot in this strange land."

Buck nodded and pulled the little scrap of cloth out of his shirt pocket. "I figgered the horse end of the yarn by this piece of cloth that got torn when the horse bucked you off, an', after seein' the horse buck, I knew you were mixed up in it someway. But how come 'em to come back after you?"

"I was supposed to go to Colfax and take the next stage south. When I didn't show up, Cash told Dave, and they started out to look for me. They knew I wasn't in favor of the robbery, anyway, and wanted to get me out of the country." She shrugged. "I don't know how they found this cabin, but they did. I thought it was you coming back and let them in."

Buck turned a cold eye on Dave James. "Why in hell did you tear up my cabin?"

The man's unpleasant face was twisted into a look of savage anger toward his sister. "She lost that damned handkerchief, an' I was afraid you *hombres* would find it an' figger out who we was."

Buck nodded. "We found it all right an' figgered out the initials." He turned back to the pale girl and it suddenly hit him like a physical blow in the chest. Her large eyes were on him and the lithesome beauty of her was wholesome and appealing. He cleared his throat as he fought for a moment's respite and forced his mind back to grimmer matters. "What's your name?" He blushed frantically and thanked the Lord for the poor light given off by the candle.

"Cyn. Cynthia James." A mantle of warm blood came into her cheeks, too.

Buck sighed audibly and his gun barrel drooped, forgotten, toward the oil-stained floor. "Cynthia, eh. I reckon you'll be needed as a . . . uh . . . a material witness against these bushwhackers."

"Yes?"

"Well, it's the law, y'know. So I'm afraid you'll have to stay in Colfax until their trial."

"How long will it be?"

He shrugged carelessly. "That depends, Cyn. Might be a week, an' then again it might take a year." He frowned thoughtfully at Rash's startled look. "The law's awful slow in these parts. Anyway, you can stay with my sister, an' I'll call every little while, to sort of drive you aroun' an' show you the country. That way you won't be bored. It's an awful pretty country, Cyn. Why, not far north o' here is the prettiest waterfall ya ever. . . ."

Rash's voice, pregnant with irony and sarcasm, interrupted sharply: "Say, Buck, remember we got a couple of prisoners here who got three thousand dollars of stage company money."

Buck vaguely heard. He was lost in the fabulous mystery of the level, warm eyes on the couch beside him. His answer was offhand and indifferent. "Your *dinero*, Colonel. They haven't had time to spend it, so I reckon they got it hid out somewhere. Prompt 'em a little, Rash. They'll tell you where it's stashed away."

He turned back to Cynthia and only vaguely heard a gasp as Rash's gun barrel was rammed heartlessly into a man's ribs. "Cyn, let's you an' me go out an' harness the buggy horse. We'll have to drive into Colfax an' get you acquainted with Tess. That's my sister. You'll like her."

Cynthia got up slowly, her eyes still holding the glance of Buck. She was breathing a little irregularly when she smiled. "I'd love to, Buck."

Rash's protesting, angry grumble came to them as they passed through the doorway side-by-side. "Listen, gol dang it, don't forget to drive back up to the house an' get our freight here." He pointed vindictively at the two sullen prisoners bound to their chairs. "They gotta go, too, y'know."

Buck nodded absently and Cynthia smiled up into his eyes as they disappeared into the shadows outside. Colonel Rash turned in monumental disgust to the notorious Dave James. "Did ya ever see anythin' as sickenin' as two people in love? Damn! Fairly turns my stomach."

James lowered his bushy eyebrows in sympathetic understanding. "Ain't it nauseatin'? I'm sort o' glad I'll be in jail where I won't have to look at all the mush they'll be droolin' over."

Cash Todd nodded agreeably. "Yeah. 'Specially since a man gets fed real food, like chili beans in jail, an' Buck'll be gettin' them indigestible things like smashed potatoes an' pie an' the like."

From down by the barn came floating back to the men in the cabin a musical laugh that rode the dingy night like a fresh blessing. Each man looked at the others, and then all three sagged sourly and shook their heads in funereal unison.

Taos Man

Chapter One

Down off the ledge of rusty, red rocks he came, lean-ing back a little in the saddle, his smoky gray eyes on the steep trail and his generous, full mouth pulled back a little against his teeth. The bay horse was head down, snorting softly as though he, too, was uneasy over the treacherous, serrated bony ribs that led down into the Santa Ynez Valley below.

Coke Bright was his name. It was a name that hadn't been heard in the Santa Ynez Valley for close to seven years. There were still some Brights in the val-ley, though, one family of them. Coke's uncle, aunt, and Cousin Jack. They were all that was left of the old stock that had come in with a long rifle and powerful back below narrowed, hard eyes, back in the early days. Time and the tide of progress had weakened the strain, robbed it of the durability and blind courage that had driven it there in the first place.

Now Coke Bright was back and somewhere, dimly in the back of people's minds, the name was musically familiar. Still, memory failing, they shrugged. Another drifter, one more hungry rider passing through Santa Ynez, staying long enough to cadge a few drinks, some meals, a little cowpunch-ing, and a few silver dollars, then he'd drift on, too, like all of the breed—always broke, restless, quiet, and efficient. All members of a peculiar, wandering tribe of men who were constantly riding on, out of the valley and into the setting sun of their destinies, never returning.

Coke put up his horse at Martin's Livery Barn. He stood aimlessly outside in the early dusk of the warm summer night and listened to the noises coming from the emigrant camp next to the livery stable. In the shadows were some huge, gaunt outlines of Conestogas. There was a smell of frying meat, sort of greasily appetizing. Nostalgia swept over the lean rider and he half hesitatingly turned toward the drab, colorless emigrants. At their fires he would find hospitality and could lose himself in the monotony of their dull conversations. Anyway, he wouldn't be lonely.

He walked among the people with their rough, homespun clothing and thick, heavy, clodhopper boots. The women were tanned with the scars of the land they had crossed, an immense, primitive land of friendliness and harshness. Kids were playing, but all the while their big, puzzled eyes watched the elders surreptitiously, showing the doubt and wonder that went on inside their heads. Coke bumped into a big, rheumy-eyed man with a rich chestnut beard. He'd been watching a girl step down from one of the high wagons.

He stepped back quickly and smiled apologetically. "I'm sorry, pardner, wasn't watchin' where I was goin'."

For just a second a fire of irritation burned high on each of the big man's cheeks beneath his baleful eyes, then it vanished. He looked at Coke's heavily silvered spurs, his sagging, worn, and ominous .45, at his careless, half-Mexican, half-Indian clothing of loose-fitting, fringed buckskin shirt worn outside a heavy pair of California pants. His eyes swept back upward to the cowboy's face. "You a native here-abouts?"

"No. Just a traveler."

It didn't satisfy the big man. Coke was obviously what he meant, whether he could put it into words or not. He frowned and shook his head. "What I mean is, you're a Westerner, ain't ya?"

Coke nodded slightly. There was a slow crescendo of loping horses, *en masse*, borne on the warm evening air and the sound of men calling to one another. Coke heard the words plainly as the riders thundered past the livery barn. "I know damned well he come thisaway. Hell, we follered his sign plumb over the summit an' even found where he slithered down them danged red cliffs. Gawd, a man's gotta be desperate to cross over up there." There was a snatch of an answer and the dusty, sweaty posse men swept past. "Yeah. You'd damned well be desperate too if you'd. . . ." They were gone and the ribbon of their hoarse voices was muffled by the other noises of the town.

Coke hadn't been listening to the big emigrant and he knew from the man's face that he'd been asked a question. "How was that, stranger? All them horses a-goin' by drowned you out."

"I said come over to my wagon an' we'll eat. I wanna ast some questions about the country ahead."

Coke sighed slightly and nodded. "I'll foller ya."

The big man's name was Hause, Karl Hause. He was from Indiana. He had a good wagon and plenty of animals to pull it, plus several head of critters that were herded with the communal flock. His wife was a raspy-voiced woman with a tremendous bosom and a jutting, indomitable jaw. She tossed a long, wavy lock of graying black hair out of her face as she poked at the smoking little cooking fire. She nodded brusquely when her husband introduced Coke. "Set."

Coke sat, cross-legged, and eased his gun thoughtfully around in front where it lay against his belt buckle. The movement was unconscious and went unnoticed by all the family. All of them, that is, except the girl who had just come around the end of the huge Conestoga wagon, a wooden water bucket on her arm. She had seen Coke unconsciously place his gun where it was instantly available and stopped in her tracks. Fidelity Hause had the rich, golden coloring of youth with a suntan. Her figure was clean-limbed, full, and firm; the violet blue eyes that were pinned on the buckskin-shirted stranger at the cooking fire were deep-set, wide, and altogether beautiful. She tossed her taffy hair and went up to the fire where her mother pointed out a spot near the cooking fire for the water bucket.

Coke moved a little, so the powerful reek of Hause's charred, stubby pipe wouldn't get in his eyes. He didn't smoke and couldn't understand how anyone else could—especially when the thing smelled as foul as Hause's pipe. He watched the emigrant's eyes and saw no sign of undue moisture. He was lost in a maze of fascination at watching the heavy, grayish clouds of smoke roll freely from the man's mouth and nose as he talked.

"We come on from Taos. You know where that is?"

"I reckon. I was born there."

Hause's ugly, rheumy, mud-colored eyes widened a little. "That so? Well, now, I hear men from Taos are ring-tailed hellers. They's a feller named Carson lives over there. Some sort of scout or somethin'. He told me. . . ."

Coke was smiling. He knew Kit Carson's uncontrollable love of scaring the daylights out of emigrants. "Carson was more'n likely spoofin' ya. He gets a big kick out of that."

"That so? Well, in that case it's a laugh on me." He removed the vile pipe from his mouth and spat a resounding stream against a massive iron-tired wagon wheel. "Now, then, young man, tell me how far's it from this here Santa Ynez to the next water?"

"About forty miles. If you're headin' west on the Oregon Trail, your next campsite'll be Chacón Springs." He smoothed off the churned-up ground with the palm of his hand and laboriously drew a crude map of the country ahead. Karl Hause was bent over, absorbed in the sketch, when some sixth sense made Coke raise his head quickly. Hause's daughter had come up and was looking at the dust drawing.

Karl Hause looked up quickly, annoyed at the interruption. He saw the stranger looking at his daughter and reluctantly took the pipe out of his mouth. "This here is my daughter. Fidelity, this here is . . . is. . . ."

"Coke Bright, ma'am." Coke was on his feet and conscious of the grease stains on his clothing and the dust on his boots. He smiled and removed his flat-brimmed hat. Fidelity saw that his hair was a sort of brownish-blond color. She nodded slightly, unsmilingly; she remembered the gun and looked pointedly at it. Coke reddened. He knew what she meant; he had heard it before from emigrants. Native Westerners were inherent killers. They were crude, reckless, and unscrupulous, like the land they lived in. She felt his hungry eyes on her and started to turn away.

Coke broke the awkward silence. "It's a big country, ma'am. It don't pay to go around unprepared." She knew what he meant and her eyes flickered over the sagging gun in its shiny holster for the quickest part of a second before she answered.

"Yes. I can see that. Also, I understand that guns are awfully handy for robbing stages and travelers, too."

Coke was stunned, and watched her walk back by the cooking fire with a startled look on his face. Robbing stages and travelers. There was some kind of an inner warning ringing somewhere in the back of his mind. He was still standing erect when he became aware of Karl Hause's voice lifted in a garrulous, plaintive sort of appeal.

"Set down, Bright. Women're always bein' nasty 'bout somethin' or th' other. Now, then, if we take this here trail to Chacón Springs, startin' at sunup, you reckon we'd git there by aft'noon, allowin' fer no breakdowns?"

"Don't see why not." Coke's frowning features were on the dust sketch, but in his mind's eye was a thoroughly wonderful, tall, lithesome figure of a woman walking away from him toward the cooking fire. He made a sudden decision and looked up at Karl Hause, who was methodically knocking out his pipe dottle against a small rock. "I'll tell you what. I'll ride with you as far as the Springs an' show you the trail from there to the Buckthorn, the next town, which isn't a town at all. It's a tradin' post for the Navajos and southern Apaches."

Hause accepted the big tin plate from his sturdy, tightlipped wife without looking up. He was plainly embarrassed. "Now, then, look here. Hell, man, you don't have to go to all that there bother. We'll. . . ."

Mrs. Hause cut him off by shoving another steaming plate past him, so that he had to lean back, toward Coke Bright.

"Thanks, ma'am."

Mrs. Hause was turning away when the frontiersman spoke. She hesitated, surprised, then threw him a quick, suspicious, but not ungrateful nod. Being thanked for anything, since leaving Indiana, was an unheard-of, unsuspected luxury.

Coke turned back to Hause. "I'll go over to the livery barn an' fetch my sleepin' gear an' camp outside your wagon." He ate in silence and the hot, thick beef gravy was foreign to his digestive tract, which had become accustomed to wolfing down cold venison and tacos or piki fixed over a bed of hot stones with, if his luck was good, a baked prairie chicken.

Chapter Two

Santa Ynez traded one kind of noise for another as darkness set in. The feverish, anxious commerce of the daytime gave way with the passing of the sunlight to a more raucous, lingering sort of bedlam. The saloons were running full tilt and the banging of off-tune musical instruments was audible over the squeals of painted ladies and rough cowmen mixed in with a sprinkling of the younger emigrants.

Coke was half asleep in the watery moonlight, the scented night air washing over him like a benediction, when a heavily shod boot came abruptly up against his ribs. He grunted and his eyes flipped open. "Easy there, pardner, this ain't no rag pile . . . it's a man sleepin'."

For a moment there was no answer and Coke looked up at the hulk of the young emigrant who towered over him. He expected to hear a mumbled apology and was mildly surprised when the stranger stooped down roughly, seized the foot of his blankets, and straightened up with a quick savage jerk. Coke spilled out onto the ground, rolled once, and was on his stockinged feet. There was just a second's hesitation, while the arrogant face before him was wreathed in a sardonic smile.

Coke Bright wasn't a tall man, nor was he especially heavily set, but he had that lithe, supple force that far outweighed either sturdiness or bulk. He minced up close and his balled up fists, white and blurred in the faint half light of the summer night, struck out venomously. The big man swore thickly, spat, and waded in. Coke side-stepped the rush, caught a brief smell of liquor and horse sweat, and fired his right fist with his shoulder down behind it. The blow caught the big emigrant flat-footed. It sounded like the crack of a drover's whip when it connected, just aft of the stranger's ear. The emigrant sagged, took two weak steps, and went down across Coke's bedding like a pole-axed steer.

Coke didn't hear anyone coming up until he heard a bull bass behind him. He spun, crouched. Karl Hause came up, carrying a swinging lantern that threw off a wavering, yellowish light. "What's going on out here?"

Coke shrugged. "Damned if I know. Some clod-hopper dumped me out of my blankets." He jutted his chin Indian fashion toward the relaxed man on the ground. "That's the varmint over there."

Hause went over, knelt down, and rolled the man. He grunted in surprise. "Hell, you've gone an' knocked Abner Larson plumb cold." There was disbelief in Hause's voice. "What'd you use? A club?" His eyes ran quickly over the silhouette of Coke's lean figure as the frontiersman opened his mouth to answer.

Another voice broke in. A soft, bitter voice with a heavy tinge of sarcasm in it. "No, Mister Bright wouldn't use a club, Father, he'd use his gun."

Coke didn't have to look behind him to know who said it, but he looked anyway. Fidelity Hause, her mass of taffy hair a faint, golden halo in the weak moonlight, stood with bitter eyes watching her father bringing Abner Larson around. She ignored Coke.

"Who's this here Larson, anyway?"

Fidelity Hause's big, violet eyes swept up to him with a flash of scorn. "He's an honest man . . . an emigrant, Mister Bright. He's what you Westerners call a clodhopper, and he's my fiancé."

Coke groaned inwardly and looked back at Larson, who was sitting weakly where he had fallen, rubbing an exploratory hand gingerly over the back of his head. He studied the big man's face and wondered what a handsome girl like Fidelity could see in the massive, coarse, harsh features of Larson.

Karl Hause got stiffly to his feet, picked up the lantern, and stood in indecision for a moment before he spoke. "We got to be out o' here with the first light o' day. Let's all get to bed."

It made sense, but wasn't particularly appropriate. Larson got slowly to his feet and pointed thick fingers at Coke. "Who in hell's that?"

Before Hause could answer, Coke took a quick step forward. "Watch your talk, clodhopper. There's a lady standin' here."

Ab Larson made a rumbling sound deep in his chest and leaned a little forward. Karl Hause stepped between the two men. "Now then, cut that out. Fidelity, you get back in the wagon." The swish of her clothing told Coke that the girl was obeying her father. He didn't dare take his eyes off the menacing emigrant, but he could picture the scornful glare the girl tossed at him as she left, and he writhed inwardly.

Karl Hause turned back to the two men and his face was wreathed in a dark frown that made his mud-colored eyes appear malevolent. "Look-a-here, you two, this thing was a mistake. Ab, you hadn't ought to fall over a man, then get hard about it." Larson didn't answer but his glowering look was sufficient.

Hause faced Coke. "Bright, you're too quick with your hands. We don't want no trouble," he spat exasperatedly. "There's more than enough grief as it is." He cleared his throat self-consciously and walked toward the wagon. "Now, then, boys, let's get some sleep."

Larson glared at Coke for a full five seconds, then spat in contempt, turned abruptly, and stalked off into the darkness. Coke lay awake for a long time, just in case Larson should come back. When he finally fell asleep, he imagined he could hear the swish of Fidelity's dress as she climbed back into the wagon.

There were six wagons in the emigrant train. They squeaked and groaned and tilted over the rough ruts of the prairie as they ambled ponderously out of Santa Ynez Valley. Coke was riding beside Karl Hause. Neither man said anything; their eyes were fixed on the twin ribbons, faint but unmistakable, that stretched like long, erratic snakes across the bosom of the raw land. Twin streaks that heralded the tide of empire. They spanned a huge, somnolent continent, and the massive, grinding wheels that rolled over them crushed out the life of the tiny, frail wildflowers that dared to bloom in the highway of progress. The morning was soft and gentle with a clear, azure sky and the faint, elusive scent of sage and sunshine spread like a blanket over the still cool prairie.

"Sure would be a good farmin' country."

Coke looked around himself in critical appraisal. He knew this land like the back of his hand, but he'd never thought of it as particularly good farm land. He shrugged. "Mebbe. If you could get shed of the Injuns an' get some water, then maybe a man could farm it."

Hause lit his pipe and the usually offensive odor didn't seem so objectionable when it was mixed with the fragrance of the sage. "The Injuns won't give us trouble much longer. It's on'y a question of time, with them." He lowered his head briefly and spat. "But the water's somethin' else again."

Coke would have argued the Indian theory if he hadn't heard a horse loping up behind them. He turned slightly and saw Abner Larson riding in beside him. Karl Hause smiled affably at the young emigrant, and Larson carefully ignored Coke.

"The boys just come in from out front, Karl. They say there's a whale of a big bunch of Injuns camped on the prairie out there."

"On our trail?"

"Yep."

Hause turned to Coke. "What you make of it?"

Coke shrugged indifferently. "Probably a migratin' band, headin' for their summer huntin' grounds."

Larson's domineering features were gravely watching Coke. "Yeah, or maybe they're out after emigrant livestock."

"I don't allow so. Injuns out here don't jump emigrant trains so close to towns. Hell, you're not more'n twenty-five miles or so from Santa Ynez."

Larson was smiling unpleasantly. "Well, I allow you oughtta know, livin' like an Injun most o' your life."

Coke tossed a wry smile at Larson and gave him stare for stare. "I reckon you're right, at that. Anyway, those of us who've lived out here know enough to stay in our own country."

Larson flushed a deep red. "You lookin' fer trouble?"

Coke shrugged again. "If you aren't all mouth, clodhopper, go for your gun."

The words were softly and quickly spoken. Karl Hause didn't have a chance to interfere. Larson snarled an oath and made a surprisingly smooth and experienced grab for his .44. He was fast, but not quite fast enough. Coke Bright's hand was jumping and bucking under the recoil of his own Peacemaker. Larson dropped his gun as his horse shied violently. He looked surprised for a fleeting second, then he slid off his mount and tumbled like a sack of wet meal to the prairie.

Chapter Three

Karl Hause looked up, ashen-faced, from the wounded man's side. "Damn. Ya almost done fer him." His hand wagged as he looked at the swollen, purplish flesh of Ab Larson's shoulder, where Bright's slug had carved a gory passageway. "Trouble. That's all we've had since we left Taos."

If he was going to say more, he never got the chance. Two things happened almost simultaneously. Fidelity Hause came running from the stopped wagons. She fell at the side of Larson, who was groaning and beginning to push himself into a sitting position. "Ab, are you badly hurt?"

Larson looked dumbly at Fidelity and amazement more than anything else shone on his face. He didn't answer. Coke wanted to be swallowed up by the hard earth at his feet as Fidelity swung slowly around, splotches of angry red on her creamy cheeks. "You killer. You aren't fit to associate with decent people."

She came up to her feet and her violet eyes were shades deeper than their natural color. "You know what I hinted at last night, and, if you'd been smart, you'd've left then."

Coke stood transfixed. In her fury she was even more stunning than before.

Karl Hause was looking doubtfully at Coke as his daughter's tongue twisted under the impetus of her anger. "Those posse men that rode through Santa Ynez spoke of you. They were hunting you, probably for some murder or robbery." Coke opened his mouth and Fidelity leaned forward and fired her final salvo as Larson got painfully to his feet and pointed off toward the west, drawing Karl Hause's attention. "I heard those men say your name. They said 'Bright's a killer,' I heard that, and now I believe it." She spun on her heel and walked away.

"There're your migratin' Injuns."

Coke yanked himself back with an effort and turned toward Larson, who, white-faced and venomous-eyed, was pointing with his good arm off toward a dust cloud. As Coke squinted into the distance, Hause threw an arm around Larson's shoulders and helped him toward the Hause wagon. Coke was left standing alone, watching the oncoming horde. He felt unsure and discouraged. Fidelity hated him. That she was mixed up, some way or another, didn't matter; that she hated him with all the animosity of her being was all that mattered. And, too, the Indians that he had so confidently guessed as migrating hunters, were a war party.

And, of course, there was the shooting. That Larson had gone for his gun first didn't seem to matter to the emigrants. He had been shot, and that alone counted. Coke leaned back against one of the massive wagon wheels and watched the Indians stop out of rifle range and study the wagon train. He was bitter and angry and didn't hear the man come up beside him until he spoke. "That means trouble."

Coke turned indifferently and surveyed the shriveled old man beside him. He was leaning on a long, delicate-looking rifle of ancient vintage. Coke nodded brusquely and looked back to where the Indians were talking among themselves. The old man's eyes were squinting against the off-center sun.

" 'Paches."

Coke took another look. The old fellow was dressed like the other emigrants. A faded butternut shirt, heavy clodhopper boots, woolen pants, and a low-topped, flat-brimmed hat. But there was something else, too, and it gave an incongruous touch to the otherwise drab individual at his side. A heavy-handled Kiowa-Apache scalping knife in a beaded scabbard hung from the sweat-stained belt at the oldster's waist. That wasn't emigrant equipment. Coke's eyes ambled back up to the man's face, and a dawning curiosity forced its way past his troubles. "Who're you?"

The narrow shoulders rose and fell eloquently and the squinted, faded old eyes swung slowly away from the Indians. "What difference does that make?"

Coke shrugged slightly and a hard grin flickered over his face. "None, I reckon," he answered, "none at all."

"Then I don't mind tellin' you. I'm Gus Hause." Coke started to say something but the old man read the question before it was out and nodded his grizzled head. "Yeah. I'm Fidelity's grandfather." He shucked a thumb over his shoulder toward the battered Conestoga behind the Karl Hause wagon. "That there's my rig." His old eyes went back to the hesitating Indians. "I been on the frontier before, in your daddy's day. I've seen those varmints before, too. Trouble, lad, trouble." He looked back at Coke. "Listen, lad. I've seen somethin' that Karl and Fidelity hain't seen. Take my advice an' kill him next time." He nodded slightly. "There'll be a next time, too, or I don't know Ab Larson." The old eyes were coldly critical as they swept over Coke. "She could do worse, at that, but she won't do nothin' 'less you open her eyes for her."

"What're you talkin' about, anyway?"

"You hain't that dumb, cowboy. Fidelity, that's who I'm talkin' about. Think I hain't been watchin' you today? You're sweet on her. All right, then, do som'thin' about it, don't jest stand aroun' every time she lights into you. Dammit, boy, give her what fer."

Coke didn't have a chance to answer. He heard the rumble of horses and looked back. The Apaches were coming in. There were at least eighty fighting bucks in the coup party. Short, stocky men with the primitive hatred of their race ingrained in their features for the transgressors before them.

Coke swung into his saddle and looked down at the old man. "Tell 'em to corral their wagons an' put their stock inside, if they can get it all in." He was gone as the old man nodded in that queer, offhand way he had. The emigrants were wringing their hands as Coke reined up beside Karl Hause's wagon. Hause and Fidelity were sitting, ashen-faced, on the high seat.

Coke felt irritation at their inactivity. "You do a helluva lot of good sittin' up there like stuffed pigeons." A little ocular resentment showed but not enough. "Get your wagons into a circle an' bring your fightin' men out." He looked straight at Fidelity. "If you got any fightin' men."

Her cheeks showed a splash of crimson. "We have 'em, Mister Bright. Not killers, just honest American fightin' men."

Coke smiled thinly. He had aroused the spirit he needed in the emigrants if they were going to make a fight of it. He nodded approvingly. "Then get 'em out here with their guns."

Karl Hause came out of his reverie with a start. The Apaches were riding in a large circle around the wagons. The noise of their cries, wild and blood-curdling, was mixed with the frantic profanity of the emigrants circling their wagons into a small, tight little oval.

Hause grabbed his rifle from the wagon and leaped into the confusion, bellowing orders in a loud, deep voice that arose above the reigning pandemonium. "Women an' chil'run stay on the floor o' the wagons. Some o' you serve as loaders. Emil, break out that cask o' powder an' ladle it aroun'. Boys, stay behind som'thin'. Them heathen'll get you sure iffen you're in sight. Take your time, boys, an' make every shot count."

Coke turned his horse loose inside the circle with the other snorting, frightened animals and dumped his riding gear unceremoniously inside Karl Hause's wagon, almost hitting Abner Larson with his saddle as he threw it over the high end gate. For a second their eyes met and Larson's held a crafty, ruthless smile. He didn't say a thing as Fidelity bandaged his swelling shoulder and he didn't have to. Coke understood Larson would kill him yet, if he could, but now he wouldn't try it with fists or guns. He'd use stealth the next time.

The Indian attack was launched with wild, unco-ordinated fury. The emigrants were white-faced and determined. There was an acrid odor of gunpowder in the clear, warm air and the defiant bellow of rifles and pistols created and sustained a clamor over which rode the screams of the Apaches, coming down the still air to the grim, embattled pioneers. Coke watched the battle with a feeling of impersonal detachment. He noted Fidelity's grandfather and father fighting side-by-side from beneath the younger man's wagon. Nothing was said as they loaded and fired with fair accuracy. He noticed two bronco bucks on the prairie beside their horses, hunkering in the grass. The Apaches were trying to kindle a fire but finally gave it up, remounted and joined their hard-riding tribesmen in the siege circle that was being maintained around the wagons. Having no rifle, Coke Bright fired infrequently. He seldom saw an Indian close enough to warrant a pistol shot.

The emigrants were giving an unusually good account of themselves. Apache warriors and horses lay in sprawled, deathly disarray, beyond the wagon circle. Coke saw an emigrant fall stiffly forward. He ran to the man, flopped him over, noted the ragged hole in his head, scooped up the rifle, and leaped into the man's vacated firing spot. He had fired and was reloading when a long, whitish sliver of wood grooved its way out of the wagon box a foot from his head. Startled, Coke ducked unconsciously and finished reloading on one knee. His charge rammed securely home, he straightened up, saw a fast-moving target, leaned forward a little to rest his rifle on a wagon wheel, and tracked the Apache over his sights. His finger was tightening on the trigger when something like a red-hot iron entered his body just above the hump of his left shoulder and ran down the full length of his left arm. The suddenness of the pain and the stunning shock of the blow knocked him a little off balance. He dropped the rifle and went down to both knees, holding the numb arm and dumbly watching the spread of scarlet through his buckskin shirt and where it dripped alarmingly from below his cuff.

Chapter Four

A sickening sensation went through Coke as he forced his attention away from the shattered arm. The smell of gunpowder, the yells of the emigrants, the angry cries of the attacking Apaches and the deafening thunder of gunfire swooped in around him where he knelt. Suddenly a leaden ball smashed savagely into the edge of the massive old wagon tire above him. He realized his peril, at the same time that it suddenly dawned on him that the shots were aimed at him directly, and were not errant slugs coming out of the maelstrom of the battle.

Rolling quickly sideways so as to achieve more protection from the marksman by gaining more shelter from the vast hulk of the old wagon next to him, Coke's right hand flashed in a blurring movement and came up with his holstered six-gun. Steely hard, narrowed eyes searched the reigning pandemonium for his adversary. Deliberately he studied the milling emigrants, the closest Apaches, and the defending riflemen. Slowly his eyes, casually, almost indifferently, flicked over the wagons themselves and he saw it. He looked twice to be sure but there was no mistaking it. A small opening in the back of the younger Hause's wagon showed the single, malevolent eye of a rifle barrel. It wasn't pointed at the Apaches beyond the wagons at all; its ugly snout was pointing across the wagon circle and downward, toward where Coke lay.

He hesitated for the briefest part of a long second. The thought flashed across his mind that Fidelity and her mother were in there. He knew who was shooting at him. Abner Larson. But still, if he fired back, there was a good chance that he might hit one of the women. Other thoughts chased themselves through his mind but he shoved them abruptly aside, figured Larson's position, and squeezed his trigger. Just before his own gun went off, the rifle jerked spasmodically, wildly, and fell out of the wagon. Coke was mildly surprised as he pushed himself to his feet and, dodging among the snorting, wild-eyed stock, made his way in a wobbly, erratic run, toward the wagon.

The high poop of the wagon was almost too much. He was trying to climb up the wheel spokes, still holding his gun, blood-soaked and slippery with the gushing elixir of his body, when Fidelity's horrified, wide-eyed face came out of the canvas.

In a flash she was beside him, ashen-faced. "Sit down. Please don't try to climb up there."

She was pushing hard against his shoulder and he sagged back to the ground, an odd feeling of light-headed sweetness sweeping through him. He didn't say anything as he sat down and leaned back against the wagon wheel. Fidelity pulled the shirt, soggy and red, off his upper body and, trembling and on the verge of actual illness, made a crude but effective tourniquet of his belt. The blood slowed and began to thicken, turning a thick, gelatinous maroon color.

Coke saw the girl clamber quickly back into the wagon and a sense of abiding appreciation settled over him as he watched the supple grace of her movements. He looked dizzily around as the sound of firing lessened. In the slowly gyrating, fuzzy perspective that had become his eyesight, a heavily beaded knife sheath dangled before him. It was an Indian sheath, and, while he felt dimly that he'd seen it somewhere before, he coupled its sudden appearance with the lessening of the gunfire and vaguely had a notion that the Apaches had breached the wagon circle. Shaking his head ponderously, he reached behind him with his good arm and tried to push himself up. The beaded sheath came closer and a strong, firm hand pushed him back down. He felt petulantly annoyed that the Indian wouldn't let him get up. No man wanted to die sitting down. The pushing, insistent hand became a huge, heavy weight and it pushed harder and harder until Coke Bright fell beneath it and slid off the side of something into a huge bottomless pit of Stygian darkness.

There were murmuring voices and the smell of wood fires and food coming into the high wagon when Coke opened his eyes. Gradually things came into focus. The high, sagging canvas of the wagon covering, gray and spotted, was overhead, the arched ribs, rubbed smooth and shiny from handling, were evenly spaced around him. He looked down at himself. He was beneath a mass of none too clean quilts and his arm was a formidable swath of pink-tinted bandages, then his eyes, stronger, swung to his left and stopped. Fidelity Hause, her deep violet eyes somber and thoughtful, was watching him. He tried to smile apologetically and a look of quick reserve replaced the frank look of worry on her face.

"Are you feverish?" He wagged his head weakly, suddenly remembering that he had shot her fiancé and wondering if she knew it. "I brought in some steak, just in case you're hungry." His eyes wandered from the thick crockery platter with the steaming meat to her white, capable hands, up her arms to the breadth and sturdiness of her bosom, beyond to the square, rounded shoulders and the handsome face beneath its canopy of taffy hair.

He smiled at the protruding, generous mouth and wide eyes. "Thanks, but I'm not hungry. What happened? I saw an Injun once, then I don't remember any more."

"It wasn't an Injun. It was Gran'pa's beaded knife sheath you saw. He helped me patch you up and put you in here. The Apaches left. They lost too many bucks, Dad says, an' couldn't breach the wagons, so they left." Her eyes fell to her hands before the unblinking admiration that shone in his glance. She started to get up.

"No. Please sit here a minute." She relaxed again and looked gravely at him. He was going to ask about Larson, they both knew it, but each had a different dread of the topic. "Larson?"

"He was killed."

Coke's heart leaped a little. Her answer hadn't shown any great sorrow, only a sort of dull acknowledgement. "What happened?"

"He was shot." Suddenly her eyes, tortured and sad, swung up and met his steady stare. "Coke, do you know who shot you?"

He nodded slightly. She must have it all. He didn't trust himself to answer and for the first time, since he had seen her there beside him, his eyes faltered. It was a distasteful subject and he felt distinctly guilty.

"I know, too." The words were slowly, clearly spoken and he looked at her again, surprised.

"Well," he was confused and wanted to soften her anguish. "I'm still around, so let's forget it."

"No, I also know something else. Do you remember when I said Westerners wore their guns so that they could rob emigrants?"

He nodded. The statements had been made in the corral yard back at Santa Ynez and had puzzled him at the time.

"Well, the reason I said it was because I overheard the posse men that rode through town mention your name, Bright, as the renegade they were looking for." He frowned a little, wondering, and she blushed. "I'm sorry, I jumped to conclusions. I met you right after that and I didn't know you had any relatives in Santa Ynez. It wasn't you, after all, it was a cousin."

He understood and smiled with relief and was going to say something when he looked up and saw the beaded knife sheath in front of him. His eyes traveled up to the leathery, calm old face above.

Grandfather Hause knelt down beside them, his face grave. "Y'know, sometimes a man has to make himself figger things out." Both Coke and Fidelity looked their bewilderment. The old man shrugged and settled himself comfortably on the rumpled quilts. "Seein' as how a man an' woman hadn't oughtta sort o' wonder about things after they . . . ah . . . set up in housekeepin', an' there hadn't oughtta be no secrets atween 'em, I just climb in here to settle som'thin' fer ya. Recollect, Coke, when you was under that wagon lookin' fer the rascal who was tryin' to kill ya?"

Coke nodded.

"Well, d'ya recollect that Larson's rifle come a-bouncin' outta the wagon just before you shot at him?" Again the nod, and the old man wagged his head slightly and tapped his own chest with a gnarled finger. "I shot just before you did. It was thisaway. I looked aroun', casual like, an' took in what was goin' on in a glance, figgered where Larson's body would be behind that there canvas, and shot him."

The old man's eyes went slowly, half fearfully toward Fidelity, who was listening with a look of vast relief on her face. She nodded slowly. "Gran'pa, I saw Ab shoot at Coke, when he was loading the rifle. I was looking for him when Ab shot at him. I was horrified, and suddenly it dawned on me what kind of a man Ab was. . . ."

Grandfather Hause's seamed old shrewd face wrinkled suddenly as he got up. "Delia, just why was you lookin' around fer this young buck, anyway?" He began to edge out of the wagon with a significant grin on his face. "Wasn't just a mite worried, was ya?" His body disappeared beyond the high seat and a musical old chuckle came back to them in the strained silence.

Coke reached out with his good hand and let his fingers cover the passive head of the blushing, confused girl. "Delia, I'm awful glad I didn't kill him."

She nodded quickly, and her eyes, dewy with a moist light, came up and met his frankly and tenderly. "So am I. It would have been something between us."

Gunman

Chapter One

Carefully, little by little, the stage driver let his gaze stray back to where Ray Kelly stood. *Time*, the driver thought, *was good to some men.* Ray stood there as young-looking as ever and unless a man knew he had been away for five years—the charge had been cattle stealing—and was either thirty years old or very close to it, he would guess Ray Kelly to be twenty-five years old, a decent enough cowboy with nothing in his background, the kind of man a fellow wouldn't mind if his daughter brought to the house of an evening, except for those five years.

The driver finished gathering the lines and pushed their loop end through the hame strap and leaned there, waiting for a hostler to come forward and lead the animals away. He made a cigarette, lit up, and smoked it.

Maybe five years wasn't really very long. To look around Welton where nothing had changed much in that time it didn't seem very long. He stole another look at the lounging cowboy. Ray was standing in the shade of Herman's Dry Goods Emporium, standing hipshot and relaxed, looking out over the town. *What ran through a man's mind at a time like that?* the driver wondered. There would be a few of the hill ranchers who would welcome Ray Kelly back; they were a pretty salty bunch anyway, but in Welton itself . . . ? The driver wagged his head guardedly. Folks were going to cut the kid off cold without a nod or a glance. There were lots of kinds of thieves in the West, but, next to a horse thief, the lowest was a cattle rustler. As the hostler came up to take away the teams, the driver opined to himself that, if he had been in Ray Kelly's boots, the last town in Arizona he'd have visited would be the one where he was sentenced to prison.

He turned, after the horses were led away, struck his trousers with his hat, and started forward toward the stage company office. A soft, hard voice hit him in the back: "You got it all figured out now, mister?"

The driver turned. "Got what figured out?" he asked that slouched, pale-eyed figure.

"Why a man like me would come back to Welton?"

The driver looked down at his feet. For a moment he made no reply, then, raising his head, he gazed squarely at the younger man. "No, frankly, I haven't." He put his hat back on. "Did it show that much?"

"It showed," Ray Kelly said. He studied the driver through a silent interval. "But then, I guess it'll be like that, won't it?"

"I expect it will. It's none of my business, but in your boots I'd have gone farther west."

"You're not in my boots."

"No."

"And I never liked running very much, pardner."

"Uhn-huh. I expect some fellers'd feel that way."

"And," Ray said, drawing fully upright and turning to glance northerly along the plank walk toward the Double Eagle Saloon, "I got a man to kill in this town before I start figuring where I go from here." He turned his back on the driver and went along the walkway to the saloon, entered without a backward glance, and approached the bar.

It was suppertime; there were only four men at a poker table and the bartender was leaning, folded-armed, upon his counter looking sleepy or bored or both. He nodded at Ray and straightened back with a sigh. "What'll it be?"

"Tequila."

The bottle came, along with a shot glass. Ray poured salt on the back of his left hand, filled the glass, licked the salt, tossed off the tequila, and tongued up the last of the salt.

"Another one?" the barman asked.

"Just leave the bottle."

"Sure. Take your time."

As the barman started moving off, Ray said: "Hold it, mister. I want a little information."

"Sure. If I can give it."

"You can. Where can I locate Mort Salter?"

The barman had a fleshy face that showed no great amount of character. Now he was looking over Ray Kelly's shoulder at someone across the room, evidently getting some kind of a signal. Finally he edged back a little with both hands still on the counter, and cleared his throat. "Well, sir," he eventually answered, "I just couldn't say."

Ray considered this, and then had himself a second belt of tequila following through with the identical salt ritual as before. Very slowly he turned his back upon the barman and looked at the poker players. They were sitting still, watching him. Each of the four cowmen was sitting erect, hands out of sight below the table, faces stonily impassive, eyes coldly, dispassionately unfriendly.

The odds were far too great; each of those men either had a palmed gun pointed barward under that table, or had a hand riding lightly upon a holstered short gun. No one, regardless of how good he might be with a six-gun, would face down odds like that, if he was in his right mind.

They knew him. He did not recognize any of them, but they obviously knew who he was, some way, and had guessed why he was back in Welton. He faced back around and picked up the tequila bottle. Well, a man who could sweat out five years on a road gang could wait another week or two with no strain. He downed the third drink, dumped a coin on the bar, and strode back out into the gathering dusk.

He rolled a cigarette, thinking that his return to Welton was not the wisest thing he had ever done in his lifetime. Those men in the saloon, for instance. They had evidently been around five years earlier when he had been tried and sentenced. They remembered him but he did not know them. He lit the cigarette. A lot of folks would remember Ray Kelly with disapproval and the disadvantage lay in the fact that he would not know who they were.

He mused over this for a while. It would not be a simple thing to find Mort Salter and kill him. By morning everyone around Welton would know he was back; they would also guess why. The odds, he told himself, were likely to become overwhelmingly great. This did not deter him but it sharpened his senses; he could not do what he had come back to accomplish alone, therefore he would get help.

Dwelling on this improved his temper a little. The mountain ranchers for whom he had cowboyed six years before would be glad to help him put Mort Salter away; they'd tried to do it a number of times themselves but had never succeeded. He made a small humorless grin in the gloom. The trouble was the mountain cowmen had never been in prison; a man learned a lot in five years of associating with the deadliest men of the Southwest.

Cooling air crowded into town off the rangeland. Welton's rough outline loomed largely against the darkening sky; the little town was beginning to stir again, evening was down and the business of daytime labor was forgotten now. Across the way men moved in and out of the Welton Hotel's supper room. Farther along the opposite plank walk strollers congregated near Russell's Café to talk and kill time before heading for the bars and poker tables.

Men strolled past where Ray stood, their voices musically soft in the deepening darkness. For a while he looked into their faces; a few he recognized but many were strangers to him. One face that pushed ahead to stop fully before him was familiar enough. In fact, he had recognized the easy walk, the wide shoulders, and the heavy bulking silhouette twenty feet away despite the darkness. Sheriff Perry Smith.

"Hello, Ray. I heard you were back."

"Perry," Kelly said in acknowledgement, adding nothing to it and biting the name off short.

Smith considered the even features and the steady, bold stare. He cleared his throat. "Had supper?"

"No."

"Care to join me?"

"No."

Sheriff Smith glanced disinterestedly up the road. "Might not be such a good idea anyway," he said before returning his gaze to Ray's face. "Folks might figure I was trying to get friendly with you."

Ray's lips drew out a little. "They'd have to be kind of stupid to think that, Perry. Either that or they'd think I forget a heap easier than I do."

"Maybe. Why'd you come back?"

"You can guess that, Perry."

"I thought you were smarter than that, Ray."

"Well, you were wrong."

"You'll never get it done, Ray. Never in God's green world. Mort's a lot bigger now than he was when you went away. He was too big for you then, remember? You don't stand a chance of a snowball in hell."

Ray's bold stare flicked over Sheriff Smith's face as he retorted: "I'm a lot smarter than when I went away, too. I've been graduated from the best school a man can walk out of . . . Yuma Prison."

"I can imagine," Perry Smith said dryly, his expression changing, the glint of his gaze firming up into a hardness. "Ray, for your own good ride on. There's nothing for you here. You can't buck Salter. I don't care what you learned in prison. He's too big for you. Another thing, folks aren't going to wait around for you to try to kill him, either."

Ray said evenly: "Meaning you, Sheriff?"

"That's right, kid. I'm not going to wait around, either. Things've been about half peaceful these last five years. You could change that if you started something. I don't figure to let that come to pass."

Ray troughed a cigarette paper, spilled tobacco flakes into it, and held forth the sack. Sheriff Smith began manufacturing a second cigarette. When Ray held forth the match, their eyes met over its dancing small light.

"Used to be some pretty good times here in Welton," the ex-prisoner said in a tone different to the one he had used up to now. "Every once in a while, down in Yuma, I'd remember those times."

The sheriff nodded soberly.

"Something I learned in prison, Perry . . . a man forgets the women he's known but he never forgets the men. You, for instance . . . I never forgot the day you come for me."

"That wasn't a very pleasant day for me, either," the lawman said quietly. "It's never pleasant to arrest men you've joked with and drank with, Ray."

"No, I reckon not. But a man's got certain things he's got to do."

"That's right."

Ray Kelly's tone roughened. "Then understand me, Perry. I've got a job to do here in Welton. It won't make it easier if I have to buck you, too. But I've got to do it anyway."

Sheriff Smith considered the glowing end of his cigarette for a silent moment, then he said: "Ray, I figure this is about the last cigarette you and I'll share." He turned abruptly and walked on up the plank walk for perhaps fifty feet, paused, threw away the cigarette, and walked on. Some cowboys jogging south along the roadway recognized Sheriff Smith and called greetings downward. Kelly heard Perry answer them out of the darkness.

He finished his own cigarette and moved outward toward the roadway, following the odor of food coming across to him from the hotel. He was hungry; the tequila had heightened and sharpened his appetite until a single urge impelled him forward. Around him Welton's night life was beginning. The sounds were boisterous, loud, and uninhibited.

The hotel supper room was not full when he found a table and dropped down, and, although he glanced briefly at the other diners, he recognized none of them. One thing, though, caught and held his attention, the women. Five years was a long time and women had had no part in those searing days and long, black, weltering nights.

He ordered his meal and relaxed. One hand lay upon the tablecloth. It was good to feel linen under one's hand, to hear the quiet voices and see the unhurried movements. He ate his meal when it came and afterward called for a cigar, a rare thing for him, and he continued to sit there enjoying the warmth, the leisure, and the peace. He even enjoyed seeing the well-fed faces around him. This would not last, but for a while he wanted to savor it. Tomorrow would be another day—the town would know him then; he wanted it to know him—but for this hour he forgot everything excepting this time of pleasure.

The weeks since his release crowded up, little raw memories of adjustments he had made, of acquiring a fresh outfit and a new gun. Of practicing for hours on end until the old speed returned, the old accuracy. Of working here and there until he had accumulated enough money to bind him over for what he had to do. Of lying under starlight with the good smell of a campfire's hot ashes in his nostrils, hearing again the sing of wind against mountain flanks and low across the plains.

A man did not return to the world of free men in a rush and all at once. It was a slow process, and, sitting there now with linen under his hand, with the sharp bite of cigar tobacco upon his lips, with the quicksilver, muted laugher of women's voices around him in the dining room, he was satisfied that the patience he had learned at Yuma Prison was a good thing, because it had seasoned him so that he could wait indefinitely amid surroundings like these, enjoying them fully while he took his time and chose the place for what he had come back to do—kill Morton Salter, if not the biggest then at least one of the biggest cow barons in Arizona.

Chapter Two

The day after his arrival in Welton, Ray rode out toward the foothills. He was not followed nor had he expected to be, but all the same he made sure before heading up through the broken country for Joe Mitchell's place. Here, where forest and hillocks and arroyos broke against the high country farther back, unless a man knew his way he could very easily become lost. Here, too, in upland parks and swales, where thick forage grasses grew, ranged the cattle of the mountain ranchers.

It was the terrain perhaps more than the people who had originally given the back country its reputation, but since then the mountain cattlemen had certainly done nothing to change things. The ranchers down around Welton lost cattle steadily and they never failed to blame the hill people. Five years earlier, it had been this condition that had brought Ray Kelly to Welton in irons, and it had been this same antagonism that had finally sent him to Yuma Prison. He had not then, knowing that for a hill rider to be tried by the people of Welton could never result in acquittal, expected anything different from what he got.

Riding loosely now, letting the livery animal pick its slow way along the trail to the Mitchell Ranch, he remembered how Perry Smith and his posse had lain in wait to catch him alone, and how Perry's ultimate success had not appeared to elate the lawman very much because Perry had known Ray was not actually a mountain cowman but was simply a drifting rider who had hired out to mountain cattle interests.

Still, none of this had made any difference. Mort Salter had sworn out the warrant of arrest and people, even then, did what Mort Salter told them to do. Ray had had five years to dwell on that one hard fact of life and he considered it now as the horse picked its way through the shafted sunlight.

Deep in the uplands finally, with the sun high above stiff-topped pines, he sought out a gravelly eminence and stopped briefly there, studying the outward slope of country southward, making his final effort to determine whether he was being followed or not. Satisfied at length that he was not, and turning slightly to gaze strongly ahead where the hills and swales gradually heightened to become gray-hazed mountains, he traced out the old landmarks. It had been, he reflected, the immensity of this uplands country that had held him there so long; he had cowboyed for Joe Mitchell for a year. Longer than he had ever before stayed in one place in his life.

Reining down off the eminence, he cut a crooked cow trail, followed it to a juncture with a zigzagging wagon path, and followed this out through red-trunked pines until it topped out over another flinty ridge and descended steadily into an immense grassy park. As the horse hip-sprung itself angling downward, Ray strained to catch sight of Joe Mitchell's buildings far off eastward, at the farthest curve of the big valley. He saw them shortly before striking level ground and eased the horse off to the right, taking a short cut away from the wagon ruts.

He had progressed less than a quarter mile when a horseman appeared through the trees to his right, jerked up sharply, and sat rock-like watching him approach. Ray neither saw nor sensed this new presence; he was thinking ahead, recalling raffish Joe Mitchell, remembering the poker games during long winter nights, the difficult roundups, and the hot, dusty days trailing cattle down to the lowlands and over to Tie Siding where the railroad dead-ended. He remembered, too, Mitchell's other riders and wondered now if any of them remained. It was not likely, he thought; five years was a long time for rangemen to stay in one place.

"That's far enough, stranger!"

Ray reined up. He felt no startlement or apprehension. Years back he had stopped others from approaching the ranch in the identical fashion. He looped his reins, kept both hands in plain sight, looked around and waited for the rider to cross out of the forest to him. Then the surprise came. He had not been stopped by a cowboy at all; it was a woman—a girl. She rode tall in the saddle without once looking away from him. She had no carbine and the holstered gun she wore was not even loosened. He could see the tie thong still secured in place holding the little pistol firmly in its holster.

"Who are you, mister, and what do you want up in here?"

He considered her for a long moment before replying. She was very handsome, much too handsome to be old Joe Mitchell's wife, and, since Joe had no children, she could not be his daughter. He relaxed, leaning a little in the saddle, his bold, steady gaze holding powerfully to her face.

"Going on to the ranch," he said, and stopped, admiring her beauty and the way midday sunlight touched her coppery hair, burnishing it to a red-gold color.

"Why?"

He made a very faint smile. "What's the difference? All you got to do is draw that little pop-gun and drive me up there, and, if I got no business there, Joe'll do the rest, won't he?"

Anger showed down around her mouth. "All right," she told him. "Ride on."

He waited for her to enforce the order, and, when she made no move toward the holstered pistol, he said: "Lady, you're going to look kind of foolish herding in a prisoner without a gun in your hand, aren't you?"

"No, mister, I don't think I will." She regarded Ray somberly a moment longer, then raised her voice to call out. "Carter, push your carbine out where he can see it!" She saw Ray's eyes locate the gun and grow still. "Now ride on," she said evenly, "and I hope you've got business in here." There was no mistaking her antagonism.

Ray took up his reins and moved out. He heard the second horseman lope up behind him but did not look around. It did not annoy him being taken like this; what bothered him was the reflection that this strikingly handsome girl was riding out with some run-of-the-mill cowhand.

They cut into the wagon ruts again less than a mile from the buildings, and here, with no shade, the heat was oppressive. Farther out lay shadows made by the rugged mountains easterly of the road and on both sides of the road were grazing cattle. They looked good, Ray noted, dark red with fat color, shiny as new money, a sight to please any range man whether he was an owner or simply a rider.

Occasionally, when an animal stood sideways, a big scarred rib brand—**JM**—stood out plain to sight. Where a hurrying creek bisected the valley and the roadway dipped to cross it, drifting cattle were strongly in evidence, either going down to drink and moving away in the tanked-up sluggish fashion of range animals returning to feed, or standing stockstill, watching the riders.

Ahead, bulking large, was the main ranch building. Around it seeming at random were sheds, shops, barns, and the outhouses found in every ranch yard. Someone was shaping metal over an anvil; each sledged blow fluted musically into the mountain air, echoing endlessly.

It was familiar to Ray, every foot of it. He headed for a stud ring bolted to a cottonwood tree near the main house, swung down, made his livery animal fast, and turned, thumbs hooked in shell belt, to gaze again at the tall girl. Her companion, about Ray's own age, was a whipcord-wiry man, lanky and free-moving, with an open and freckled face that looked across at Ray with none of the girl's obvious antagonism.

"Go on in!" the rider called to Ray. "Joe's either in there or somewhere around. I'll see if he's out here some place." It was said in a conversational manner, not as though the cowboy was suspicious of Ray.

The girl looped her reins and moved across the yard, her spurs stirring snakeheads of dun-colored dust. "What's your name?" she asked in the same impersonal, inflectionless, cold tone.

Ray turned deliberately away from her without answering and bent a long stare upon Joe Mitchell's old log ranch house that stretched, long and low, across the yard. Behind him the girl's indrawn breath, knife-like with quick hot anger, sounded distinctly.

Ray crossed the porch and struck the door with his fist. Beyond, somewhere within, came sounds of movement, then the panel flung back and a short, compact grizzled man peered up at Ray from a face as eroded as the mountains around that weathered log house.

"Hello, Joe."

"Well . . . hell! Well . . . I'll be a . . . Ray Kelly! Son, come on in here!"

Ray was literally jerked into the house and at once its smoky odors touched him, bringing up nostalgia. He freed his hand finally from the older man's grip and wiggled the fingers ruefully. Joe Mitchell's strength was legendary in the mountains. So were his hospitality, his generosity, and his temper. Equally as legendary were his principles; no one in the mountains, or down around Welton, either, for that matter, had such elusive principles, and Ray had never doubted but that old Joe Mitchell shipped short year-lings from time to time whose blotched JM brands covered older marks. But a young cowboy imbued only with love of life and excitement could laugh at something like that; it was knowledge to keep a man warm during chilly nights and to amuse him during days of sweat, dust, and swearing, when trail boredom and roundup *ennui* would otherwise have sparked the restlessness that prompted riders to move on. But a man nearing thirty did not laugh so readily over rustling, particularly a man who had just spent five years in prison because of it.

"Damn, boy, but you look good." Mitchell's little

probing eyes danced; his face threatened to split wide open from smiling.

"You haven't changed any, Joe."

"Ah," the cowman said, pointing to a chair. "When a feller crowds sixty, he can't change a whole lot . . . unless it's to up and die. Nature's put about all the lines in this face there's room for."

Ray sat. His heart warmed to Mitchell in spite of something in the back of his mind. He began thoughtfully to twist up a cigarette. Not because he felt the need, but to cover up a very faint uneasiness that had accompanied him into the house.

"Want a drink, son?" Mitchell called out in his booming voice.

"No thanks, Joe."

Ray smoked with his hat on the back of his head. Nothing in the room had changed—those wide black smoke stains on the front of the huge fireplace; the bedraggled Indian feathers on a moth-eaten old warbonnet hanging in a corner; the dust and dirt that obscured details in a framed picture of U.S. Grant.

"You figured I'd come back, didn't you, Joe?"

"Sure, kid, sure. I knew that as sure as I knew anything. I got a place for you, too. You knew I'd keep a bunk waiting."

"Joe?"

"Yeah?"

"For five years I've wanted to ask you just one question."

Mitchell stared fully at Ray and began nodding his head. The levity died away, the heartiness. His tone turned steely, and this was the Joe Mitchell that Ray remembered best, the smiling, steady-gazing Joe Mitchell who would spit in a mountain lion's eye using this brisk voice, or who could laugh uproariously at a practical joke in a cow camp across the mountains. This was the Joe Mitchell who stole cattle or went into a gunfight; this was the real Joe Mitchell, the man who really lived behind that bluffness, that heartiness and raffish smile. You didn't work for a man twelve months, eating out of the same cooking tin with him every day, and not know what was behind the mask of his face.

"I'm waitin', Ray."

"Did you rustle those cattle from Mort Salter they sent me to prison over?"

"No, son, I didn't."

They exchanged long stares and beyond the house, muted now by log walls, the sounds of a struck anvil rang out. Then Ray removed his cigarette, crushed it out, and smiled.

"Sure good to be back," he said simply.

Mitchell arose. "Come on. I want to show you 'round the place. Five years is a long time. Things've changed a heap on the ranch."

Ray got up. "Joe, a girl got the drop on me a mile out and brought me in like I used to do. Who is she?"

Mitchell's tawny gaze flicked upward in a twinkling look. "Son, that's Grace Fenwick. You're fixin' to meet her pa. He's my foreman now. Been on the place little over two years."

"You're softening up," Ray said, still not moving. "You used to say a cow outfit was no place for women."

"Getting old." Joe chuckled. "Come along. I want you to meet George Fenwick . . . her pa. He's a widower, and, when he come along with the girl . . . well, hell . . . you know me, son. I hire a good man when I see one." Mitchell opened the front door and lounged in the opening. "Ray, men live an' learn. The trouble is some things you learn too late. Like havin' women around a ranch. Grace keeps the boys spruced up. You'll see at suppertime . . . no spurs in the house, no guns wore at the table, no shaggy whiskers. Even clean shirts once a week." The raffish eyes turned sly. "Pretty as a picture, too, isn't she?"

"She sure is."

"Well, son . . . you're last in line."

"I'm not even in the line," Ray drawled, recalling the girl's look of pure dislike and taking up his hat to follow Joe Mitchell out into the sun blast.

Chapter Three

It was George Fenwick in the blacksmith shop, shaping up shoes for a big, wise-looking, raw-boned chestnut gelding, who was banging on the anvil. He stopped to draw back and wipe his hands on the leather apron when Joe and Ray entered, and Ray saw immediately where the girl got her height, her auburn-copper hair, and her wide gray eyes. Joe Mitchell introduced them and Fenwick's grip was solidly powerful. He did not smile, though, and listened gravely as Joe explained who Ray Kelly was. Finally he said—"Yes, I've heard about you."—and that was all.

This, Ray thought privately, is a man no one gets close to, and he accordingly was as sparse of words as the foreman was.

"Grace brung him in," Joe said, grinning from ear to ear.

"Not exactly," Ray corrected him. "There was a rider with her. Someone named Carter. He backed her up with a carbine."

The big man near the anvil lifted one half of the split apron he wore and finished wiping his hands upon it. Ray thought, just for a second, a shadow passed over Fenwick's face.

"Carter Wilson," Mitchell said, and to Ray Kelly who knew Joe well, it seemed that Joe was not fully at ease in his own blacksmith shop. Then the moment passed and Fenwick was speaking.

"Well, I'm glad to have met you, Ray." He glanced at the patiently waiting horse. "Now I've got to finish this job. . . ." He waited, and, when Joe said nothing, he nodded brusquely, and turned his back.

Out in the yard again, Ray said carefully: "Joe, whatever happened to Duncan Holt who used to be foreman when I worked for you?"

Mitchell's gaze muddied a bit, and, when he answered, he ignored the question completely. "When you get to know George, he's not a bad feller. He's not a man who makes a good impression right off, but he grows on folks. You'll see, son." He touched Ray's arm, turning him. "Come on over to the bunkhouse. We'll stake out your bed."

Here, in the log-insulated coolness of the one room above all others on a cow ranch riders remembered most clearly in after years, nostalgia hit Ray hardest. When Joe pointed to an empty lower bunk and said—"That's yours."—Ray recalled without effort the shock-headed, good-natured man who had formerly occupied that bed.

"Tower Houston used to bed down there," he said.

Mitchell nodded, gazing downward. "Tower's gone, kid. Got killed in a brawl over at Tularosa couple years ago."

Ray counted the war bags tied to each bunk. "You got only five riders now, Joe?" he asked, thinking that in other days the Mitchel Ranch had employed ten full-time men and during drives and roundups had hired an additional five riders temporarily.

"Don't have as many critters any more," stated Mitchell, passing back out into sunlight. When Ray caught up, Joe was smiling again, but it was not a spontaneous or even a pleasant smile although it tried to be.

"Joe. . . ."

"Yeah."

"Maybe I'd better not work for you again."

Mitchell was clearly not surprised by this and had not yet come to a conclusion in his mind about something, for now he said: "Plenty of time to go into that later, Ray. Look after your livery barn critter and wash up, if you're a mind to, and sort of amble 'round the place. I'll see you at supper. Afterward we'll talk."

Ray watched the older man move off toward the main house. *Something is wrong here*, he told himself. *Something has cut some ground out from under Joe Mitchell.* This intrigued him, for to his knowledge there was no better cowman in the whole Southwest than Joe Mitchell, and there was no trickier character, either. If something was getting the better of JM's founder, it had to be something other than another man. At least, Ray thought, heading for his horse, it had to be something other than an *ordinary* man.

He put up the animal, forked it a bait of mountain hay, and strolled down to the creek. Behind him afternoon sunlight slanted down across Mitchell Meadow, reflected backward from the saw-toothed easterly mountain range, and there was a great depth of silence over everything.

Nailed to a tree was the warped old washstand he sought. Some things never change, he thought, taking up the basin, dipping low, scooping it full from the creek, and bending forward to wash. He could almost hear the catcalls and laughter of riders crowding up around this spot after long days under the summer sun. Tower Houston, he remembered particularly, because he was now dead. Duncan Holt, Cuff Wayne, Jack Martin, Rick Richards. . . . He pulled out his shirt tail and dried his face, blinked ahead, and grew very still. Fifteen feet away the girl, Grace Fenwick, was watering her horse below the washstand and boldly studying him. He pushed the shirt tail back into his waistband and returned her look.

"You could have told me who you were," she said.

He nodded. "I could have. I guess I really should have, ma'am."

"But you wanted to put on an act."

"No, ma'am, it wasn't that." He finished with the shirt, combed his hair with bent fingers, and replaced his hat. "You see, a long time ago I used to bring strangers in just like you fetched me along. It kind of tickled me . . . being brought in that way myself. And another thing, ma'am, when you've been gone a long time, you ride along remembering things. Your mind's not exactly cheerful."

"Five years," she said. "My father told me."

He rummaged her face for reaction to the knowledge that he had been in prison. There was nothing to be read there; she was totally impassive except for her eyes. They were entirely impersonal; she might have been regarding a new horse or an earmarked but unbranded calf, something out of the ordinary but of no immediate importance.

"For rustling," he said, driving the words out.

"I reckon Joe told you things've changed at JM since you went away."

He thought there was an undercurrent to her tone and withheld his reply, turned cautious by her steady gaze. "We talked a little," he admitted. "Joe seems about the same, though."

"He isn't. Not like he was when you worked here."

"Meaning, ma'am?"

"My name is Grace. Everyone calls me that."

"All right, Grace. My name is Ray Kelly. Folks call me Ray. About Joe . . . ?"

"He can tell you. It's his business, not mine."

He eased forward to sit upon the washstand with one leg dangling. "Joe and I've been friends a long time, Grace. We've done a few things together."

"I can imagine," she murmured dryly.

He ignored that. "He used to have a good bunch riding for him, too. No 'punchers who hid in the trees while girls rode out to challenge strangers."

"That was my idea, not Carter's!"

"Doesn't change anything, Grace." He began working up a cigarette. "I guess things have changed around JM." He lit up and inhaled. "Doesn't seem to me like they've changed for the better, though."

Anger showed in her eyes and her voice was swift when she spoke again. "Ray, I think you'd better ride back where you came from." Her voice was cold. "There's no room on JM for your kind any more."

"No?"

"No! And I'll make sure you do ride on, too!"

"How, ma'am, with that little gun?"

She stood rooted a moment longer, then wheeled, pulled the horse around with her, and strode quickly back toward the yard.

Ray continued to sit on the washstand, smoking, while she was still in sight. She was uncommonly handsome even in anger. Or maybe more so because she was angry. His thoughts returned to their conversation. Something was wrong all right and, whatever it was, was right here on JM, too. He turned a little, somberly watching the creek rush past, clear as newly spun glass with scurrying, erratic trout minnows in it and the gravelly bottom glistening.

"Mister. . . ."

He turned. It was Grace's father. He no longer wore the shoeing apron but his sleeves were still rolled up disclosing heavily corded tanned forearms.

"Mister, I think you'd best saddle up and get along."

There was no mistaking the hostility here. Ray eased up off the washstand and dropped his cigarette. Inside him something primeval stirred, the blood quickened in his veins, objects became sharply clear in his vision. This man, instinct told Ray, was ready to fight.

"If Joe tells me to ride on, I'll go," he answered evenly, "but what you tell me doesn't mean a damned thing, Fenwick."

The big foreman continued to stand motionlessly, gazing fully forward. "I've been told you were the fastest gunman Joe had, in the old days. But that isn't going to make any difference, Kelly."

"No," said Ray. "Not when you're not wearing a gun." He raised his eyes from Fenwick's middle. "Why'd you take it off? You had it on in the blacksmith shed."

"Because I didn't want this to end with one of us getting killed. But you're going to ride on all the same." Fenwick took several short steps closer to Ray.

"You've got Grace right well trained."

"She didn't have to tell me anything. I sized you up the minute I saw you, Kelly. You're a gunman. You mean trouble."

Ray was watchful, but more than that he was puzzled. "Tell me something, Fenwick. What's going on around here?"

"Nothing. This is a cow outfit. It's being operated like one. We don't raid the lowland herds. I've heard how things were run when Duncan Holt and the likes of you worked here, but my deal with Joe Mitchell was . . . no rustling. That's why I'm telling you to ride out."

"You know," Ray drawled silkily, "I came back here to kill a man who called me a rustler. I'd just as soon kill two men for calling me that as one man."

"Not an unarmed man!" Fenwick exclaimed.

"Go get your gun then."

"No."

"Then start whatever you've got in mind or make it plain you weren't calling me a cow thief just now."

There was a shine in George Fenwick's eyes; he was going to fight and that knowledge passed to Ray Kelly. Fenwick squared himself up, then lunged, one big, scarred fist whipping upward. Ray stepped in closer, not away, caught Fenwick around the middle before he could draw down the upflung arm, and raised him bodily off the ground, bent far back, and heaved the foreman against the ground.

Fenwick rolled over and got up. He shook himself, and moved in again, tried a feint that did not succeed and crouched, moving cat-like around Ray's left. The younger man turned easily, pivoting on his toes, waiting. Fenwick's face was expressionless. He threw a long overhand blow that missed, then sprang forward. This time Ray, recovering his balance after ducking away from the overhand strike, could not get clear. Fenwick struck him high in the chest, then twice, lower, in the soft parts, and Ray took two big backward steps and two more sideways. Fenwick went past beating air.

Ray let the opportunity go; his stomach was

knotted with pain. He sucked in great gulps of air and slid away as the foreman recovered and came back in again, swinging. Then he ducked low, dug in his toes, and jumped. Fenwick was oncoming and could not avoid collision. He struggled against the clawing hands trying mightily to save himself. Ray caught hold, pushed his face into the older man's chest to protect it, and, when Fenwick was bending forward, Ray stiffened his legs with a sudden and powerful upright spring, the top of his head cracked against the foreman's jaw, and Fenwick sagged. Ray let go and jumped clear. Fenwick's eyes were awry.

Ray moved beyond reach, arms down and waiting.

"All right," a new voice said thickly, brimming with excitement and hostility but trying to be impersonal, "you made your point, Kelly."

Ray turned. It was the man who had brought him in with Grace Fenwick. Mitchell had called him Carter Wilson. He came forward from the shadows heading toward Fenwick.

"George, you all right?"

Fenwick's muddled brain was clearing, but he was still unsteady on his feet and a trickle of flungback blood showed across one cheek from a split lip. "I'm all right," he muttered, touching his mouth. "Kelly. . . ."

"Forget it," Ray said between sucked-back deep breaths. "I'm staying." He caught up his hat and walked away.

Out where the afternoon sun smash was hottest, he found Grace standing near a corral in the shade of a shed and went across to her.

"Thanks," he said, sharp enough in his tone to bring her swiftly around facing him, and with the smoky look of battle still in his gaze. "Next time you'd better send two of them instead of one, though. Never send a boy to do a man's job." He started to move off.

"Wait!" She had paled. "What did you do?"

"I didn't shoot him . . . I just knocked him a little fuzzy-headed is all."

"I don't believe it!"

"Well, go down there and see."

"You couldn't. You're not man enough to whip my dad!"

Ray considered her through an interval of silence, and then he said: "Lady, a man like your dad learns to brawl in saloons and bunkhouses. That's where I learnt, too . . . but the first man I fought in Yuma Prison whipped me in less than ten seconds. After that I found out that barroom brawling is for kids long on guts and short on experience. A place like Yuma Prison teaches a man a lot of things. One of them is how to fight, and fight to win."

He left her staring after him, crossed to the main house, and pushed on inside without bothering to knock. "Joe!" he called. "Joe, where are you?"

Mitchell came hurriedly from a back room, drawn by the whiplash of that calling voice. He stopped in the doorway. "What the hell happened to you?"

"Nothing much, but your foreman's got a headache."

"George . . . ?"

"Sit down, Joe. I can't wait until after supper for our talk."

"Ray, there's nothing to be sore about," Mitchell

protested, but he crossed to a chair and sank down. "A little misunderstanding . . . those things happen, son."

"Joe, Fenwick's girl hates my guts. That's all right. I never cared much for women, either. But she prodded her pa into jumping me at the creek and I left him wobbling around down there. Now what I want to know is who he is, what he's doing giving the orders around here, and why he ordered me to saddle up and get out?"

Mitchell's face changed expression several times in the space of seconds; it colored slightly and the cowman looked away from Ray to the wall, the floor, his hands, and back to Ray again. "Sit down," he eventually said. "Sit down, boy, and relax. I'll tell you what you want to know."

Chapter Four

"About three years ago," Joe explained, "I began losing cattle, Ray. Someone was comin' up in here and rustling them out of the parks. I hired more hands and we patrolled. It didn't do any good. I still lost 'em. I got the other mountain ranchers to help me patrol and still I lost cattle." Mitchell's moving glance grew still. "I know it's hard to believe, son, but we never caught a single rustler . . . not a blessed one."

"How could they work that?" Ray asked. "You know the parks better than anyone else."

"It took me nearly a year to find out how they worked it, Ray." Mitchell fixed the younger man with a stare. "Can you guess?"

"No," Ray answered promptly. "You had a good crew. They moved the cattle, patrolled the trails. If it was the same bunch of boys I knew at the JM, there wasn't a better bunch of riders in the country."

"That part of it's right enough," agreed the cowman. "With one exception."

"Who?"

"Tell me something, Ray. When you were down in Welton did you run into anyone you knew?"

"Perry Smith is all. Why?"

"None of Salter's crew?"

"No."

"Then you don't know who Mort's foreman is?"

"No."

"Duncan Holt!"

Ray was jarred. Holt had been the JM foreman when he had worked for Mitchell. He knew him well, had in fact been on many a drive and roundup with him. Duncan Holt had always been as loyal a man as he thought existed. Joe spoke again, scattering Ray's thoughts.

"Duncan put the herds where he wanted them. He led the night patrols. Salter's boys rode up to where Duncan had ranged the cattle and drove them off. It worked real good because Duncan always patrolled a long way from where the herds were hit. You understand now?"

"Yes," Ray mused, "but . . . Duncan?"

Joe nodded. "I lost nearly three thousand head, then Duncan quit me, and the next thing I knew he was Mort Salter's range boss. Summer before last I went down to the bank at Welton to see about borrowin' some money to buy replacement cows with and they turned me down. Mort was one of the directors at the bank. Afterward he took me to the saloon and laughed in my face."

"He told you . . . ?"

"He told me, boy. Bragged about the whole thing."

"Did you go see Perry?"

Mitchell shook his head. "No. I rode out with my crew to Salter's range. We spent two days goin' through his herds. Ray, there wasn't a single solitary dog-goned JM critter among 'em."

"What'd he do with 'em?"

"I'm not sure but rumor has it he traded them south of the border in Mexico for unmarked Mex critters and had the new cattle driven up, re-branded, and turned loose on his range."

Ray's thoughts of his fight with George Fenwick

were gone. He sat still looking at the older man. Outside, several riders loping into the yard made a familiar sound in the hush.

"We used to pick up a few slicks now and then," he said finally, "but we never stole any cattle, Joe."

"I know. But we were mountain cowmen, Ray, and. . . ."

"Joe, you know why I'm back in the country?"

"Yes, I know. But I don't think you stand a chance. That's what I aimed to tell you tonight after supper. Mort's almighty big now, boy. Far too big for you to handle."

"It isn't just that I want to even things up for those lost five years, Joe."

"No?"

"No. Listen, a man does a lot of figuring in prison. He gets some conclusions and he rides them right out to the last notch."

"Sure, kid, but. . . ."

"Let me finish. The thing that kept puzzling me in Yuma was that no evidence was presented against me, Joe. If I'd stolen those cattle, what did I do with them?"

Joe shrugged, holding his silence.

"That's why the first thing I asked you when I got back was if you'd stolen them."

"It wasn't me, Ray. I give you my word on that."

"But someone stole them, Joe, and not a single hide showed up as evidence at the trial. All the same I was sent to prison." Ray leaned suddenly forward in his chair. "That's what I mean," he said, strong conviction in his tone. "I didn't steal them, you didn't, no hide nor hair of them ever showed up anywhere in the country afterward, but Salter proved by his tally count and his books that he'd lost them, and he had five witnesses who swore they'd seen me driving them off. That's what kept stickin' in my craw in prison. I could figure everything just that far, Joe, and no further. Now I think I've got the answer."

"All right, what is it?"

"Salter stole those damned cattle from himself, sold or traded them down in Mexico, got me railroaded into prison, and made a pile of money for himself at the same time."

"But . . . why you?"

"I was handy. It could've been any of your crew. Salter's hated your guts for years. That's no secret. He's told folks you're a cow thief so long now everyone believes it."

"Ah," Mitchell said, "a few slick-eared calves now and then. Hell, if we hadn't gotten them, some lowland outfit would have."

"Salter would have, Joe, but we were a better crew and he hated us for that, too." Ray got to his feet. "I figured Salter stole those cattle from himself some way. I thought about it a lot and that was the only logical thing I could come up with." He looked down at Mitchell. "Now you understand why I'm going to kill him, don't you?"

"Well . . . not exactly, Ray."

"Not for sending me to prison altogether, Joe. For making a fool of me. For bragging around Welton how he'd caught himself a simpleton and railroaded him into prison."

Mitchell looked glum. "You'll never get it done. You've been gone five years and Mort Salter's bigger now than any two cow outfits in the country. Not only that, but if he knows you're in the county, he'll put a price on you, Ray. Someone'll blow your head off before you get within a mile of him."

Ray relaxed; for some indefinable reason he felt good. Now he smiled down at Mitchell. "Like I told Grace, a man learns things in prison he couldn't learn anywhere else. If Mort gets me, at least he'll know he's had a run for his money."

Mitchell stood up, crossed to a window, and looked out. The sun was sinking in the west, shadows were puddling out in the yard, and down by the log barn men were forking hay to corralled horses.

"It won't help you any," he said over his shoulder to Ray, "if you give Mort a scare and die doing it." He turned facing Ray. "I don't think you can count on much help, Ray." He said this reluctantly, his eyes sliding away from the younger man's face. "I better tell you something," he muttered. "Fenwick's my foreman all right, son, but the bank at Welton put him up here."

"What?"

"You see, this year the bank let me have that money to buy replacement stock with. . . ."

"Go on."

"Well, I had to agree to hire Fenwick so he could supervise the herds, Ray. Otherwise . . . no loan."

"Why didn't you tell them to go to hell?"

Mitchell sighed, crossed back to his chair, and dropped down. "Listen, Ray," he said very earnestly, "I've fought off Injuns and blizzards and varmints . . . and I've got as good as I gave from rustlers until Duncan like to broke me . . . but cow ranching isn't just fighting any more. It's running a business, dealing with bankers and such like, and I'm 'way past the half-century mark and this new fangled finance and what not sort of throws me."

"Joe," Ray asked thoughtfully, "did you agree to keep Fenwick until the money is paid back?"

"Yes. Like I just said . . . if I hadn't, they wouldn't have loaned me the cash."

"One more question . . . did Fenwick ever work for Mort?"

"No, leastways he said he never had." Mitchell leaned back. "George is all right, son. You may not work double with him but he's a good man just the same. Thing is, he's dead against picking up slick-ears and dogies and unmarked critters of any kind. He's pretty dog-goned straight-laced but he's a good cowman."

"Hell!" Ray exploded. "If you don't try to even up your losses on a mountain cow ranch by marking unmarked strays, Joe, you'll lose every dog-goned calf that's dropped out in the mountains some place to other outfits."

Mitchell continued to sit there in the deepening shadows saying nothing, looking past Ray toward the window.

"Joe? Did you hear me?"

"I heard you . . . but I don't ride any more, Ray, and George runs things now."

"Then get rid of him and. . . ." Mitchell's gaze fell across Ray's face, silencing him briefly. He scowlingly began manufacturing a cigarette. When it was going, he spoke again. "All right, you can't fire him. Then keep him on and let me have part of your crew to work the high country, Joe."

Mitchell seemed to consider this before he said: "Kid, there'd be nothing but trouble if I did that."

"Since when has Joe Mitchell ducked trouble?" The younger man demanded hotly. "Joe? What's got into you? Hell, five years ago we had JM humming."

"It was a different crew then. Duncan was. . . ."

"The hell with Duncan. Let's get JM running like

a cow outfit again, Joe . . . then we'll look up Duncan and Mort."

"It's Mort's got the mortgage I had to give the bank to borrow that money, Ray. I dassn't antagonize him or he'll wipe me out." Mitchell pushed up out of the chair. "Ray, like I said, I'm not a young man any more. I don't want to end up living in a tarpaper shack down in the gulch behind Welton while Mort Salter winds up with JM. I'd rather just go along George's way and get the loan paid off."

"George's way," Ray said caustically. "How long will that take? Hell, Joe, you'll lose half your calf crop every year, running things his way. You'll never get that loan repaid."

chapter Five

It was beyond six o'clock, nearing seven in fact, when Ray left the house heading straight across the yard for the corral. The riders were not in sight when he caught the livery animal, flung his saddle across it, and stooped to catch the cinch. He heard voices down by the creek and through his indignation it came to him that Joe's hands were down by the washstand getting spruced up for supper. Three deft flips and the latigo was looped up snugly. He was dropping the stirrup again when Carter Wilson came forward out of the evening and stopped when he saw Ray saddling up. Wilson blinked, then nodded and shuffled his feet.

"Leaving?" he asked.

"Yes."

"I see. Well . . . maybe it's best."

Ray turned his back to bit the animal. Wilson continued to stand there watching him. When Ray finished and turned, the cowboy said: "George'll breathe easier, anyway."

Something in the rider's tone made Ray pause. "So will his daughter!" he exclaimed. "So will Joe, I think."

"I reckon," Wilson said in the same thoughtful way. "I reckon it's best all around, except for one thing."

"What's that?"

Wilson was balancing something in his mind. He finally lowered his voice so that the words traveled not farther than the barn doorway. "Don't take the south trail down out of the mountains, Kelly." Then he moved, heading back out of the barn.

Ray dropped the reins and lunged forward, caught Wilson just beyond the opening, and whirled him around with one hand. "Why not?" he demanded.

Instead of replying, Wilson put up a hand and pushed Ray back inside the barn out of sight. Then he dropped the hand and said swiftly: "Because George sent one of the boys off right after you whipped him and I got the notion someone's going to dry-gulch you as you ride back down toward Welton."

"Why?"

"Darned if I know . . . except that maybe George don't like being butted in the mouth."

"That's no reason to kill a man."

"Maybe. Maybe not. Who knows how a feller feels about things like that?" Wilson started forward again, and Ray arrested him once more.

"Why are you warning me?"

"I just don't like the idea of fellers getting dry-gulched, that's all. I got no reason to like you, either, but if I wanted your scalp, it'd be out in the open." Wilson pulled free and walked swiftly out into the lowering evening.

Ray got astride the horse and rode across the yard, down across the creek, and up along the crooked road. He rode slowly and loosely, thinking of George Fenwick and Joe Mitchell. About Joe there was little to consider. Of the people he had known five years earlier in the Welton country, Joe had changed the most, and it had been a bitter thing to stand there in Joe's house and see how much the cowman had changed.

As for Fenwick, he had not struck Ray as a dry-gulcher. He had, in fact, left an entirely opposite impression, he was not a man who believed in a loose rope or a running iron, and he had made it very clear. Then how could Wilson, who must have known him better than Ray did, think he would try to get Ray killed?

Tentative understanding did not come for an hour. Not until Ray was cutting southerly into the forest a long mile east of the regular trail down out of the mountains. Fenwick did not intend to get him ambushed, but Wilson obviously knew something Ray had only just guessed. Fenwick reported the arrival of strangers on the JM to Salter. Salter, Wilson must also know, was not above having a man dry-gulched.

He came out on a limestone ridge and halted to look and listen. There was no sound of pursuit, and, as far ahead as he could see in the limited evening, nothing moved. He urged the horse forward over a twisting, unused old game trail.

What a mess Joe Mitchell had gotten himself into. It was difficult to believe it could have happened to Joe, who had never, to Ray's knowledge, been equaled as a cowman and as a loose-rope artist.

He got safely down onto the plain north of Welton without seeing or hearing anything unusual, struck out for the town on ahead, and made good time as far as some old buffalo wallows before halting again to listen. This time he heard riders, but only briefly, then they, too, stopped. He smiled thinly; this was not a game he had not played before, the pursued and the pursuit riding the night by sound. He waited fully five minutes before the horsemen started forward again, and he moved out, too, riding with his head cocked for the next stop they would make, and bending far to his left to avoid contact, for the horsemen were approaching from the direction of Welton.

It took two hours to accomplish it but he finally lost them, and rode on into town, put up the livery animal, and went to the hotel for a room. The desk clerk handed him a key, waited until he disappeared up the stairs, then scuttled out into the night.

Beyond the solitary window of his room, Welton glowed with orange lamplight. For a while he stood looking out and smoking. Riders jingled past and strollers on the plank walks slow-paced the night finding in night's coolness relief from daytime heat. A fist rattled across the door and Ray spun around.

"Who's there?"

"Perry. Open up."

He crossed to the door and drew it back. The sheriff entered without looking up, went to a chair, and dropped down. He bent a long, critical look upon Ray.

"Dog-gone you, anyway," he growled. "Who'd you think that was out there north of town?"

Ray's face brightened. He almost smiled. "Was that you? It sounded like a posse."

"It was a posse, damn it, and I was leading it. We were looking for you."

"I haven't done anything."

"Yet," the sheriff said bitterly. "I wasn't after you, Ray. I was simply trying to prevent you from being put on ice."

"Oh . . . ?"

"Word came this afternoon that Salter knew you

were back and had put a thousand dollars on your head . . . dead."

"How'd you know where I was?" Ray asked.

Perry looked pained. "Do I look simple-minded? When the liveryman told me you'd left town, I knew where you'd gone, dog-gone it. You'd have gone up to see old Joe yesterday if the stage hadn't pulled in late." Sheriff Smith removed his hat and dumped it on the floor beside his chair. "Listen, Ray, you've got to leave Welton. I'm sorry but that's it . . . you're to pull out and not return."

"Who says so?"

"I do."

"That's not good enough. You're drawing to a busted flush. An old poker player like you knows better than that. I haven't done anything . . . haven't broken any laws."

"Like I said . . . not yet. But I can still jail you. I'll call it keeping the peace."

Ray eased down upon the edge of the bed. For a moment he did not speak, then he said: "I'm not going, Perry, and you're not going to jug me, either. Last night you said we'd shared our last cigarette. Well, that's all right with me, if you want it that way. If Salter's paying your wages, too, then I'll just have to avoid you. But I'm not pulling out. I didn't intend to yesterday, and today I've got more reasons than ever to stay?"

"Such as?"

"For one thing a fellow named George Fenwick."

"And?"

"Joe!"

Sheriff Smith took up his hat, turned it in his hands, and regarded the uneven sweat stains. He got up out of the chair and raised his eyes to Ray's face. "You're going to get killed," he said, making the words into a statement of fact.

"I doubt that, Perry, but, if it happens, I'll tell you one thing . . . Mort Salter'll be lying right beside me."

"That," the sheriff growled, "was a tomfool thing to say. You're going to get killed before you even see Mort Salter again."

"By you, Perry?"

Smith's face flushed darkly. "He doesn't own my gun and you know it."

"Then who's going to down me?"

"Don't be so dense. Mort's got two of the fastest guns in the Southwest on his payroll. He's also got fifteen doggoned tough riders working for him who'd try anything for a thousand dollars. If that's not enough, every saloon bum in Welton'll be lyin' in an alley, waiting for you to show your back." Smith put on his hat and tugged it angrily forward. "Did they teach you how to live through odds like *those* down in Yuma?"

"That," exclaimed Ray, also arising, "is exactly what they taught me!" He crossed to the door and held it open.

As the lawman went forward, he said with hard finality: "Ray, if you're still in town come morning, I'm coming after you. And *not* because Salter's got his hand on my shoulder, either. Simply and solely to keep the peace."

Ray closed the door and leaned upon it, thinking. Perry Smith, he knew, did not bluff, and, despite the coldness now existing between them, Ray had no fight with the sheriff.

He thought, too, of the information about Mort Salter's gun hands Perry had dropped, and this, he told himself, was going to be just as hard as everyone said it was going to be—this shoot-out with Mort Salter. He returned to the window and resumed his speculating there where cool night air came across Welton's rooftops to leach away the tiredness that was beginning to seep into him.

Later, he rolled up two blankets off the bed and went back downstairs. At the desk he threw down a $5 bill, exchanged a smoky stare with the clerk who he deduced correctly had informed the sheriff he was at the hotel, got no argument at all, and strode outside, across the roadway, and into the livery barn. When the night man shuffled up, he told him to saddle his toughest horse. While that was being done, he rolled the blankets, and afterward lashed them behind the cantle, handed the hostler some coins, and stepped astride.

Beyond Welton he cut easterly across the range, riding with both familiarity and wariness. A $1,000 bounty was, as Sheriff Smith had intimated, a strong incentive. One day back in Welton and the fire he had known his return would spark was raging. He smiled coldly and took the measure of the ugly, ewe-necked buckskin ridgling he was riding. If a mean little eye, a hammer head, and a sloping rump meant anything, he had exactly the mount under him he would need. Not simply for his present ride to Salter's Rafter S Ranch, but for the chase that was sure to follow.

There was no moon this night and the stars were dimmed out by rising heat waves from the plain that obscured their wet brightness. It was a good night for manhunting, providing the hunter knew where to find his man.

Easterly, bulking large against the lighter murk of sky shadow, loomed a mountain range. Northerly, also, solid blackness carved chunks from the fainter horizon. Where the range flowed a rusty yellow, there was only to be seen that which lay immediately ahead; a man had to know his destination this night and know it well, or he could ride in a circle until dawn.

Somewhere on ahead a swift fox yapped, evidently catching the scent of an oncoming horseman, and farther along a rodent-hunting owl that was skimming low veered frantically with beating wings, frightened by the looming fast-walking rider.

Past midnight Ray slowed to listen, not expecting to hear anything really but making no mistakes, either. He was then within sight of the Rafter S and by dismounting, lying flat and looking upward, could skyline the cottonwoods, the ugly squareness of blackened buildings, and feel within himself that sharp sting that inched out along a man's nerves when he was closing in on the kill.

He left the horse anchored to a stump less than 100 yards from Salter's buildings and glided forward as far as the bunkhouse. There he paused before attempting the long trot across Salter's yard toward the main house. There was no other way to get where he wanted to be than by crossing that clearing, and, perilous as this was, he did not think now, so late at night, the danger was very great.

But caution on the part of the hunter is often less than the fear of the hunted; he did not see the dark shadow rise up off the ground on his right until he was twenty feet from the house, then the quick discord of a gun being cocked in all that stillness was as loud almost as the actual firing and Ray flung himself sideways and downward at the same time.

A flash of flame came fractions of a second ahead

of the explosion and the bullet sang past. Ray was rolling when he fired back, twice, heard the carbine fall, and afterward saw the sentinel's body curl to the ground. He sprang up and ran hard back where he had left the buckskin ridgling, threw himself pantingly into the saddle, and whirled away. Behind, the Rafter S yard was boiling with men whose weapons glinted evilly in that vague, weak light.

Chapter Six

By daybreak he was back in the mountains considerably north and west of the JM and hungry enough to eat a bear. He knew every foot of the country around, and, although there were several ranches not too distant, he did not head for them to get food for the simple reason that, if Salter had succeeded in humbling Joe Mitchell, Joe's neighbors, he thought now, would also be intimidated. If this was so, they would certainly hear soon enough that Ray Kelly was back and they would also hear of the attempt by someone to break into Salter's house. It would require no great genius to deduce who had made this attempt, and, when Salter's men came into the mountains as they surely would now, if the upland cowmen knew where Ray was, they might inform against him. It was hard for Ray to believe Salter had been able to intimidate those mountain cowmen until he reflected on Joe Mitchell for a moment. Afterward he decided that if Joe could be harassed, the other mountain ranchers could, also.

He had no trouble locating an empty meadow where the buckskin horse could stand knee-deep in red-top and recoup, but the problem of provender for himself was a different matter. He dared not shoot game, and, after he had fashioned a number of snares, it was a long wait before they produced anything. He filled up on tobacco smoke and sought out a rocky bluff to lie upon watching his back trail and the distant, murky plain north of Welton. There was nothing to see even after the sun was riding high, but when it approached the zenith, he sighted a lazy dust banner beating onward toward the foothills. He smoked and watched.

The riders were coming from the east; they would be Salter's men. They struck the first lifts with the sun directly overhead and faded out in the broken country and tree cover. Seven of them and every man armed to the teeth. Ray smiled to himself, returned to his park, gathered two valley quail from the snares and one rabbit, made a dry-oak fire that gave off no smoke, and cooked his first meal in the uplands since returning to them. After that he slept.

With evening well advanced, he finished what had been left from his earlier meal, saddled the tough buckskin, and leisurely started easterly through the mountains until he sighted Mitchell Meadow. There, he pressed onward, skirting the open country until, hours later with darkness fully down, he came in behind Joe's log house. He smoked a cigarette there, with the buckskin dozing behind him in the tree fringe, and waited for the bunkhouse lights to die. Then he went quietly forward, came down behind Joe's house, groped for an open window until he located one, slipped over the sill, and cat-footed it forward through the stillness of the house.

Joe was in bed. When Ray roused him, the cowman sat up and reached for a lamp at the bedside table. Ray stopped his hand. "We don't need light to talk by," he said. "It's Ray."

Mitchell sat up straighter. "Boy," he whispered, "you sure kicked a hornet's nest this time. What the devil did you try and assassinate Mort for anyway?"

Ray let the question go past unanswered. "What did his men want up here this afternoon, Joe?"

"Want? Why, what'd you expect them to want . . . you, of course. They knew you'd head for JM when you got back into the country."

"What did you tell them?"

"Nothing. I didn't know much to tell them, son. You were here and you rode off. They wanted to know where you might hide out. I said I didn't know, which was the truth."

"Anything else, Joe?"

"Yeah," he answered dryly, "they said Mort sent me word that, if you made another try for him, he'd clean me out lock, stock, and barrel." Mitchell reached for his shirt, rummaged for a tobacco sack there, and began twisting up a cigarette. "Got a match?" he asked, and, when the smoke was rising, he said: "Kid, I thought you'd know better'n try something as risky as ridin' into Mort's yard like that."

Ray, smelling the tobacco, made a smoke of his own. "I didn't intend to kill him, Joe. Not really, but I wanted him to think I was going to."

Mitchell exhaled. "You succeeded," he said succinctly.

"Was Duncan with the men he sent up here?"

"No. His men said Duncan was bringing up a drive out of Mexico."

Ray's eyes brightened with interest. "Did they say where he was now, or how long he'd been gone?"

"One of 'em said Mort'd sent Duncan word somewhere down by Tanque Wells about you bein' back in the country."

"Tanque Wells." Ray got off the edge of the bed. He was thoughtfully silent for a moment, then he nodded. "Joe, did Mort's message scare you?"

Mitchell scratched his head, rumpled his hair, and screwed up his face before replying. "Something you younger fellers don't know!" he exclaimed. "When a man's getting up in years, he don't scare too easily. Like I told you before, Ray, I don't want to end up in a shack behind town like a saloon bum, so I walk soft where Mort Salter's concerned . . . 'specially since he's got me roped and tied with his bank . . . but scairt? Nope, son, he didn't rightly scare me." The raffish eyes lifted. "We know each other pretty well, boy. You ought to know old Joe Mitchell might keep the peace a mite . . . but he don't run scairt from any man."

Ray made a wolfish smile. "Then I want you to do something for me."

Mitchell's gaze blanked over and his eyes left Ray's face. "What?" he demanded.

"I want you to help me bust Mort Salter."

"How? You know . . . if you fail, you'll be dead, but I'll be worse'n dead. You thought on that, haven't you, boy?"

"I've thought on it, Joe. I also know it's a sight better being dead than livin' on your knees, too."

Mitchell considered. He smoked a moment in absolute silence. "I never heard it put that way before," he said. "Go on. What am I supposed to do?"

"Get word to Mort you saw me down near Welton with five ridge runners, all as hard-lookin' as any gunmen you ever saw."

After waiting a moment Joe said: "Is that all?"

"For now, yes. Will you do it?"

"Sure, that's not much of a chore." Mitchell, whose spotty background had included a little back-trail riding, grunted. "You'll have to be awful careful, Ray. Mort'll have spies out all over the country now."

"I'll be careful, don't worry about that."

"They'll be watching JM from now on, too. You figured that, haven't you?"

"Yes."

Mitchell fixed the younger man with his shrewd gaze. "Have you really got friends ridin' with you?" he asked.

Ray shook his head. "No. I want Mort to split up his men."

"I see. I reckon you don't want to tell me any more'n that. . . ."

Ray was moving off when he said: "That's right. What you don't know no one is going to sweat out of you, Joe." At the doorway he paused. "I'm going to raid the kitchen for a bag of leftovers, Joe. Don't get a chance to drop in at restaurants riding like this."

"He'p yourself, son." Mitchell put out his cigarette. From the room's darkness his voice sounded slightly louder now. "George's girl hung around here tonight after the boys had eaten and headed for the bunkhouse, son. She was full of questions about you."

"Oh . . . ?"

Mitchell pushed down under the quilts. "Funny thing about women. Sort of like green colts. If you rough 'em up a little, they seem to respect you more'n if you gentled 'em."

Mitchell was watching the lanky silhouette with his appraising glance twinkling a little. He expected Ray to ask questions but the younger man stood silently still without saying anything for a moment longer, then faded beyond the doorway.

Ray filled a flour sack half full of tinned foods and left Mitchell's dwelling as he had entered it, by the window. The yard beyond was without movement.

For a moment he considered the little log house set slightly apart which was the foreman's residence, before heading out for the forest fringe where the buckskin was waiting.

It took a little time to wrap the flour sack in a blanket to disguise its whiteness, and then he untied the buckskin, turned him once before mounting after the custom of all experienced riders, and started to raise his left leg.

"Hold it!"

He grew stiff, recognizing that he had been taken by a wily gun hand. The safest time to brace a man on the run was when his left hand had the reins and mane in it and while his right hand was curled around the saddle horn preparatory to swinging up; both his hands were as far from his gun as they could be.

He eased the foot back down, kept both hands in plain sight, and turned. It was too dark among the trees to make out his companion, but he could make out the highly polished shine of a pistol barrel, and it was that sight which made him relax.

This gun barrel was not blued; it was nickel-plated. Only one person on JM that he had encountered carried a little nickel-plated short gun.

"Well," he said irritably, vexed at being caught like that by a girl, "you going to stand there all night? You got me dead to rights. I'm not going to make a play."

She moved out of the darkness slowly, displeasure visible on her face when she stopped less than fifteen feet from him. "Was that all you stole?" she demanded, flicking the pistol's barrel toward the rolled bedding behind his saddle. "No money?"

The darkness hid his quickly mantling angry flush

when he answered her. "No money," he drawled in that deadly tone. "And if you were a man. . . ."

"Don't let that stop you," she snapped across his words, firming up her grip on the pistol.

He sucked in a big lungful of air and let it out in small pinches. They stood there regarding one another like bristling dogs taking each other's measure, thinking thoughts, discarding them, and considering fresh ones. Ray had never before looked upon a woman as a man's equal in a showdown, nor did it occur to him now that he was considering her in this light although he definitely was; she was, at least for this moment, his match, this tall lithe girl with her uncommon beauty and her bitter, flinty stare.

"Why did you come back?" she asked coldly.

"For food," he replied, deciding that since she thought he was no more than an outlaw, he would let her go on thinking that to protect Joe Mitchell. But he saw immediately that she was his match here, also.

She shook her head at him. "Not likely. You passed other ranches getting up here. Just for once try telling the truth."

His anger came up again. "That is the truth," he said in that same very mild tone.

"Part of it," she said. "What is the rest of it?"

"That's enough for you," he snapped.

She studied his face. "I can guess the rest, Mister Kelly. Now tell me why you didn't take the regular trail out of the mountains when you left JM?"

"How do you know I didn't take it?"

"Because I followed you . . . that's how."

"All right," he said thinly, "I'll tell you. Because after I whipped your pa, he sent word to Salter I was in the mountains, knowing Salter'd set up an ambush and try to get me killed."

Something dark moved into the background of her stare and flamed out at him there. "You're a liar! My father never had a man dry-gulched in his life!"

"Ask him," Ray said stonily, feeling pleasure over having jarred her. "Ask him if he didn't send out word I was here."

"He may have done that," she said. "You're an ex-convict, an undesirable, but he'd never send word to anyone to shoot you down."

"Listen, Grace, when a man sends word to Mort Salter an enemy of his is in the country, he's signing someone's death warrant. You'd never convince me you're naïve enough not to know that much about Salter."

"My father is an honest man!"

"Maybe. I don't know him that well." Ray smiled; he had her on the defensive and meant to keep her there. "I'll tell you one thing about him, though . . . he sure can't fight."

He saw her heavy underlip grow thin with pressure, her eyes turn smoky in a smoldering way, and her blouse rise and fall with the dull rhythmic slugging of her heart and knew he had touched her where doubts lived.

"Before you take me," he said, his voice turning quiet and normal again, "tell me how you happened to find my horse up here in these trees tonight?"

"I didn't find him here. I heard you riding north around the valley when I went for a walk after visiting Joe tonight. I didn't know who it was, but I didn't think it was one of our boys, so I kept back a ways and trailed you on foot. When I located your horse, you were already gone. I waited." She suddenly lowered the gun, letting her arm drop back to her side. "You can go," she said, gazing steadily at him. "Go on . . . ride off."

He was puzzled and made no move toward the horse. "You aren't going to take me in . . . ?"

"No."

"Why not?"

"That's my business. Just mount up and head out." She spun, and, before he could speak, call her back, she disappeared through the trees. He mounted slowly, forehead puckered in thought, and reined slowly away from JM, riding south.

Chapter Seven

From the JM down past Welton to the neighborhood of Tanque Wells was sixty miles. A long ride at any time without a change of horses, but in the darkness it was even longer. Ray was cautious only as he skirted around Welton; afterward, he pushed the buckskin horse as hard as prudence dictated, conscious that he would also have to rely on the tough and ugly animal to bring him back to the mountains again.

He had only two advantages over the man he sought. He knew where Duncan Holt would be, in a general way at any rate, while Holt would not know where Ray was, and the second advantage was that he rode only at night, using the darkness as his friend and ally.

Dawn of the first day out found him deep in the eroded desert country between Welton and Tanque Wells. He made for another water hole, not as large or popular as the Tanque, which suited him perfectly, and there he hobbled the buckskin to graze upon sparse bunch grass while he slept. The blasting midday sun awakened him with its pitiless burning. He washed, drank deeply, took his carbine, and walked out as far as a barren rise to study the country ahead and behind. There was no sign of movement in any direction. He ate some beans, smoked a cigarette, and waited with that peculiar depth of Indian-like indifference to the passage of time he had acquired at Yuma Prison for the sun to set.

He also thought, and the thing that kept returning to puzzle him was Grace Fenwick's refusal to take him back to her father. Had she been fearful for him or had she been afraid that what he had told her was the truth, and considered him less important than the truth about Mort Salter and her father?

There could be no answer, he knew, until he talked again with her, but this did not hold out any promise of pleasure; he was, without thinking of it in that light, again viewing her as he might have considered a man. She was dangerous to him, and, while he acknowledged to himself that she was beautiful, this was no part of what existed between them.

The sun eventually dropped westerly in a reddening way, sending burnished banners dagger-like across the sky. Shadows crept out from beneath chaparral bushes and rocks, short and fat at first, then drawing out longer, thinner, as the light of day faded still more, and over everything was the strong, acrid desert scent, the yielding up by the earth of a great, silent sigh as the heat lessened, a time of hush and blessedness and coming coolness redolent with an odor of creosote bush, of peyote, and cooling rocks. It was as pleasant to a man who had not smelled it as the stronger fragrance of the uplands, equally as missing from his life for the past five years.

He was in no hurry and therefore lingered a while longer, enjoying a desert sunset before saddling and riding southerly again, down the long, broad corridor of badlands beyond which lay Mexico, speculating on the manner of Mort Salter's dealing below the border. He could, he thought, find out how Salter operated in Mexico, but it would take more time than he liked to think of spending south of the border. Furthermore, in the end it was not relevant to his plans, and finally he had an idea anyway, from what he had learned at Joe Mitchell's place.

Salter, in the past at least, had rustled cattle from cow outfits around Welton, blamed the thefts upon the mountain cowmen, then had either sold or traded the stolen beef deep in Mexico where the likelihood of discovery was nonexistent, and in this fashion had grown both wealthy and powerful. It was, Ray thought as he threaded his way down the night, a simple enough operation, one that would appeal to the Mexicans, and in the end, because he also knew Mexican cowmen, he was riding now to implement a notion that he felt sure would disrupt Salter's operation and greatly amuse—and enrich—the Mexicans.

Around seven o'clock Ray started easterly where the north-south cattle trail lay. At nine o'clock he cut the trodden pathway and swung southerly along it, riding easily and carefully. He considered it likely that Holt's herd could not be far below him.

The land heaved away beneath a moonless sky in a kind of broken and irregular monotony of brush, boulders, and arroyos of no great depth. Far back and dimly discernible against starshine stood the mammoth mountains of the uplands, higher and therefore blacker than anything else in this dead world of stillness and silence. On ahead there was nothing but desert, but by ten o'clock Ray scented cattle, and shortly afterward he heard them. Not loud or even continually bawling as driven animals would do, but lowing with weariness, with dumb-brute protest as though bedded down for the night.

He dismounted when the sounds and smells became sharper, tested the air for direction, then went forward afoot until he saw distantly the briefly swelling glow of a cigarette tip, then its gradual ebbing. By lying flat he could make out the hard cut of a mounted man's shape against the skyline. He got back to his feet and very carefully circled the bedded herd, searching out additional riders.

There was a small fire burning low where horse shapes stood thickest, and fitfully exposed, when the fire sparked, were the lumpy shapes of four sleeping men upon the ground.

He walked nearly a mile back out away from the bed ground, mounted up, and sat thoughtfully still for a while. He had been unable to locate Duncan Holt but knew there were six riders with the herd. He estimated the cattle to number close on 700 head, and, reflecting upon the kind of cattle they were, he knew they would stampede readily enough, trail-weary or not. He knew this because of the distance Holt's night hawks kept between them and the herd, plus the view he'd had of a few wicked-horn steers standing guard, keening the night from time to time with raised heads, on guard. He smiled to himself, unlimbered his handgun, balanced it lightly for a moment, then urged the buckskin horse forward.

He came down on the bed ground from the north in a choppy lope and fired the first shot while still 500 yards out. His second shot lanced the night when he was only 100 yards off and into its shattering echo came the loud click of horns as cattle sprang up in alarm. After this shot, too, came the angry protest of Holt's men near the dying fire. They were also springing up.

Out of the west a horseman loomed, suddenly calling a hard curse forward. Ray spun away as this man rocketed ahead, short gun dimly shiny in the gloom, angry enough to fire but reluctant to do so. It took a moment to shake this hard-riding wraith, and, when Ray cut loose the third and fourth shots, he was coming directly in upon the herd from the east.

Two thunderous explosions so close to them started the cattle crashing forward into one another and within a matter of seconds the desert quivered from charging hoofs. Now Holt's men no longer held their fire; the stampede was on and nothing but gunshots could quell it, but even a few shot critters dumped in the path of their fear-maddened companions did not ordinarily stop a cattle stampede in the dark.

Over the gunfire and the roll of nearly 1,000 panicked cattle came men's thin yells from time to time as Salter's crew sought to stay along the flanks of the herd to hold contact until the beasts had winded themselves. Ray was there with them, pushing the buckskin close and firing over the backs of Salter's orry-eyed Mexican critters that were heading as straight as an arrow back for the country where they had been raised.

Not until he heard a familiar booming voice calling for the men to drop back, to let the cattle run themselves out, did Ray veer off, loping easterly to be clear of discovery. A half mile out he drew down to a walk, letting his mount recover its wind. He reloaded his gun and holstered it. Far ahead but clearly audible was the powerful reverberation of stampeding cattle. He finally halted, seeking to pick up the sound of shod horses; he knew that Duncan Holt, experienced as he was, would not wear out horses trying to stem that red-backed tide, but in the interim would certainly waste no time in seeking the gunman who had caused his present dilemma. Reining farther easterly, Ray thought it helped considerably, knowing your enemy.

He was not through yet, though, and on the dawn side of midnight pushed southerly until he located a few run-out critters nosing through the chaparral. He left them to search out the main herd, and, after finding it and satisfying himself that the cattle had recovered their wind, he charged out of the night a second time, firing and yelling like an Indian, effectively starting a second panicked stampede. This time, with no riders close by, he got the cattle well away before turning off, reversing his course and starting at a rapid walk back northward again.

He had accomplished what he had hoped to achieve; it was a long way back to Mexico but some of Salter's herd, perhaps a third of them, would return to their former ranges, and, if Salter recovered them, since it was not the practice to trail-brand herds for so short a drive, he would have to buy them back, and this would gratify the Mexican *rancheros* equally as it would enrage Mort Salter.

Additionally, since the herd was badly scattered, Salter would have to keep at least six riders searching for them, and this was primarily what Ray wanted to accomplish. It would lessen the odds against him from fifteen to one, to perhaps something like nine to one, still rather great odds but, by whittling, he expected to lessen it considerably over the next few days.

By daybreak he was back at the isolated water hole again. There, he left the buckskin to graze and drowse, took his flour sack of food to the sentinel knoll he had used the evening before, and alternately slept, ate, and kept watch for riders heading back toward Welton with the news for Mort Salter of what had happened to his herd.

Late in the afternoon, before sunset, he struck out for the uplands again. A little short of midnight he passed far to the west of Welton, heading leisurely north toward the foothills, but he stopped shy of them when the night came alive with the faint echo of swiftly moving horsemen, waited until the sound had diminished far behind him, then skirted the hills westerly for nearly ten miles before cutting up into the depths of shadows that hid him completely, and there, with pine needles muffling the sound of his passage, he bore steadily to his right until he got back to the high mountain meadow he had ridden down out of several evenings before to have his talk with Joe Mitchell.

The buckskin horse badly needed a rest and he got it. For three days Ray lazed in the quietly fragrant highlands, making a few sorties afoot in the direction of JM, finding grim satisfaction in the number of riders who passed in and out of the mountains now. The evening of the fourth day he slanted back down to the plain heading for Mort Salter's cow range. There, as he had expected, he found heavily armed cowboys patrolling both the foothill approaches and, southerly, the open country leading away into the desert. Salter, he thought, was expecting another raid. It was obvious by the strong force he was posting to prevent it that Salter, thinking as a rustler would think, considered it likely Ray would hit his herds hard in a second attempt to drive his cattle down into Mexico.

He drew back into the foothills, off-saddled, and reconnoitered the country behind him, waiting for sunup. When the first rays came of a fresh, new day,

he had his retreat figured and dozed fitfully until the
day crew loped up to relieve the night men. He sat
there idly, carbine across his lap, watching the riders
and the grazing cattle, and not until mid-afternoon
did he see what he was waiting for.

Twin spirals of dust hung heavily in the wake of a
swiftly moving, wheeled vehicle far out. When the rig
was closer, sunlight flickered off spinning wheels.
Ray got up, smiling. If you knew how a man thought,
you could anticipate him, and a man who had spent
five years with rustlers and outlaws knew how such
men figured.

He led the buckskin behind him into the longest
spit of forest where it thrust forward a short distance out onto the range, and there he rested the carbine in a tree crotch. The range was too great, he had
known it would be, but what only Ray Kelly, of all
the people who knew he was back in the country,
was certain of at that moment was that it was not his
intention to assassinate Mort Salter at all.

Five years had added some girth to Morton Salter.
It had also enabled him to dress exceedingly well
and it had paled his skin. Ray could make out these
details if he could not see Salter's bloodless lips, his
hot and vicious glare as he climbed down from the
buggy, but from memory he had no trouble at all recalling them.

Several riders loped forward to halt where Salter
stood. Two of them dismounted and the burly rider
who had driven up with Salter stood, wide-legged
to one side, gazing past where the cattle grazed.

Salter, Ray could see, was upset about something. He gestured when he spoke and his body was
hunched forward as though bracing forward in anger.

Ray waited, finger curled, eyes steady down the

barrel, and, when several of Salter's riders moved back toward the horses, leaving an opening, he fired, levered and fired again, withdrew the gun swiftly, sprang into the saddle, and tore out through the trees. Distantly, out on the plain, came the wild calls of men and the quick, hard slam of riders pelting forward toward the foothills.

Chapter Eight

Ray's latest strike against Salter, being a personal one, beat up a storm in the country. From his upland lair he watched posses of Salter's men pass to and fro between the range and the mountains. They did not appear to be searching for him as much as they seemed to be patrolling the known trails leading to Joe Mitchell's ranch.

His success also had repercussions in other quarters; some of the upland cowmen, who had formerly avoided JM so as not to become embroiled with Salter, were emboldened now to ride to JM, seeking a way to join the fight. When Joe told them he did not know where Ray was nor where he might strike next, they seemed not to believe him, but, against the possibility that Joe might see Ray again, they left word that Kelly would find fresh horses, food, ammunition, and men willing to ride with him, if he chose to visit Joe's neighbors in the mountains. Ray, of course, knew nothing of this. He dared not visit JM although he wanted to, because, while unafraid of being caught himself, he could imagine Salter's reaction if it came out Joe had talked to Ray.

Finally there was another repercussion to all this. Sheriff Perry Smith, under pressure from Salter, rode himself lean hunting a wraith he did not expect to find, which failed to improve his temper any, thus, when he was riding alone toward JM and Ray eased out of the forest to confront him, Perry Smith's first word was an uncomplimentary one.

"Damn you," he growled by way of greeting. "I told you there'd be a ruckus stirred up if you didn't ride on."

Ray, eyes twinkling over the sheriffs dourly acid expression, kept a hand hanging loosely beside his six-gun. "Why blame me?" he asked mildly.

Sheriff Smith regarded him hostilely a moment before answering. "Who else should I blame? Now, listen. . . ."

"Sheriff, let me get my two bits in first, before you start preaching."

"There's nothing you can say and you know it." Smith relaxed in the saddle, darkly scowling. "You took a couple of shots at Mort, you stampeded his herd down near Tanque Wells, and you shot the leg out from under one of his men in his own dog-gone yard."

"Sheriff," Ray said finally, "do you want to arrest me for those things?"

"I not only want to, Ray, I'm going to!"

"Do you have any witnesses who saw me do any one of those things, Perry?"

"Witnesses?"

"Sure. The last time I was tried in Welton there were five witnesses who swore they'd seen me steal Mort's cattle. If it hadn't been for them, I couldn't have been convicted because there was no physical evidence introduced." Ray's smile dwindled. "There won't be any physical evidence this time, either, so you've got to have witnesses. You got any?"

"No," Perry said shortly, "but Mort'll find some."

"Like he did last time?"

Sheriff Smith cleared his throat before replying. "Listen, kid. . . ."

"I quit listening five years ago," Ray interrupted. "No one talks me into anything this time." His eyes, brightened now, turned as cold and hard as steel. "But I'll go back with you, Perry, voluntarily. I only ask one thing of you . . . after I'm disarmed, you give me your word I won't be cut down in your jail or taken out and lynched by Salter's hired hands."

The sheriff had begun to frown before Ray was half finished. Now he said: "What's in your mind, Ray? You're not doing this because of conscience or anything like that?"

"There's something in my mind, sure, but like I said . . . this time I'll play out the hand my own way."

Smith looked past Ray. "You figuring on having your friends bust you out?"

"What friends? I'm alone."

"Not the way I heard it you aren't."

"Salter tell you I had men with me?"

"Yeah, he said you couldn't have stampeded those cattle by yourself nor taken shots at him unless you had men to cover your trail."

Ray chuckled. "Take my word for it," he told the sheriff. "I am alone in this. But it's good to know Salter doesn't think so. I want him to think, after I'm in jail, there might be others who'll be gunning for him."

Perry Smith's long face was thoughtful. "You're taking it for granted I won't tell him otherwise," he said.

"I don't think you will, Perry. Not after we've had a long talk in your jailhouse."

"What kind of talk?"

"Perry, I never told you I didn't steal Mort's cattle, did I?"

"Well, not personally, no. But you said that at the trial."

"I think I can explain to you what happened to those cattle. If you're as honest as I think you are, you'll check me out on that."

Smith frowned. He removed his hat, peered into it, and replaced it. He had misgivings and they showed. "Listen, Ray," he said suspiciously, "I'm not aiming to get sucked into one of your crazy schemes and made to look the fool afterward."

"You won't look like a fool. I promise you that. But before we go, I want your word about protection."

"That," said the sheriff offhandedly, "you'd have anyway. No one takes prisoners away from me, and Welton hasn't had a lynching in ten years."

"It might now, Perry. Mort's money can buy an awful lot of whiskey."

Smith's face turned hard-set. "Not that much," he opined evenly. "A shotgun has a pretty soberin' effect, too." He sat there a moment in silence, then he said in a different tone: "Ray, I'll take you in, but I'd sure feel easier in my mind if I knew what you were up to."

"Nothing illegal," the younger man replied, raising his rein hand, urging his horse out in a walk. "Let's go. I get a funny feeling between the shoulder blades sitting out here in the open like this."

Sheriff Smith reined around and they struck out. Around them midday sun smash glittered evilly in a lemon-yellow way and beyond sight but squatting low upon the dancing plain Welton drowsed in the heat. Ray rode with moving eyes; he knew Salter's riders would be abroad if scarcely anyone else was—

a $1,000 incentive would more than offset 120° heat to men whose lives had inured them to inconvenience.

But they made it to Welton without trouble, and Sheriff Smith put Ray in a cell, tossed Kelly's gun on his desk, and pushed back his hat. "Hot," he said to the prisoner. "Hotter'n the hubs of hell. I'll fetch you a bucket of water."

When he returned, entered Ray's cell, and deposited the bucket in a corner, he said: "The town's comin' to life. The ones who saw us ride into town went and roused everyone else." He straightened up, looking squarely at Ray. "Boy, if you'd just ridden on. . . ." He left the cell, locked the door glumly, and was turning away when his prisoner spoke.

"Perry, if I'd ridden on who would have been next?"

The sheriff faced around, looking perplexed. "What are you talking about?"

"Salter. If I'd ridden on, who would he have railroaded next?"

"You haven't convinced me he's railroaded anyone yet."

"But you know he owns the bank now."

"What of it?"

"And that he's got Joe Mitchell roped and tied."

"Joe's no saint. He's gettin' about what he deserves."

"You're the sheriff, not the judge," Ray said. "Draw up a chair and we'll have our little talk now."

Smith teetered, a moment undecided, then he got a chair, was in the act of dragging it up when a light rap echoed from the front door. He let go the chair, drew up briefly, and then moved forward.

"It won't be Salter," he said over his shoulder. "He'd have come through that door like a wild bull."

It was Grace Fenwick. The sight of her standing there turned Ray to stone, Perry Smith was equally nonplussed, but he stepped back and closed the door, barred it after she entered.

"Ma'am," the sheriff mumbled. "Mighty nice to see you." He gazed steadily at her, waiting.

"Can I see your prisoner?" the tall girl asked.

Perry did not move. "You live a long way out," he said softly. "How'd you know I had a prisoner?"

"I saw you arrest him."

Perry blinked and behind him, from the cell, came Ray's soft laugh. "Sheriff," the prisoner called, "you didn't know you had a white Indian in your county, did you?" Smith turned, frowning. "She sees everything, Perry. There's nothing much goes on that girl doesn't know." Ray's smile lingered; he returned to Grace Fenwick's gaze. "You knew where my camp was?" he asked. Grace nodded without speaking. "Why didn't you lead Mort's men to it?"

"That's why I'm here," the girl replied, her voice turning a little sharp. "To ask you some questions."

"Fire away, ma'am."

"First, who told you my father sent someone to Salter after you and he fought?"

"Afraid I can't tell you that, ma'am. Not that I wouldn't ordinarily, but I don't want to get a man killed."

"He won't be killed. As I told you, my father. . . ."

"I wasn't thinking of your father," Ray said swiftly. "I was thinking of Salter."

"Then tell me this. Did you know you did exactly what Mort Salter wanted you to do, when you let the sheriff arrest you?"

Ray shot Perry a glance before replying. "I came in with both eyes open," he said.

"Do you know there's a reward on your head?"

"I know that, ma'am," Ray acknowledged. "Tell me something," he said. "Why didn't you turn me in?"

"Because," the girl answered frankly, "I'm not sure you stole those cattle you were sent to prison over."

"Oh?" Perry Smith said, eyebrows climbing upward. "Can I ask you why you doubt it?"

"Joe Mitchell told me some things a few nights back."

"Such as?" Sheriff Smith insisted.

Grace did not answer immediately. She was gazing straight past the bars at Ray. Finally, vaguely she said: "A lot of things. I asked my father about them. I also listened to the men talk. Then I began watching you, Mister Kelly, and. . . ."

"And?" Ray prompted.

"Well, I'm not sure, but I think Mort Salter is not quite what my father and a lot of other people think he is."

"You'll have to do better than that," the sheriff said dryly, moving toward., the chair in front of Ray's cell. "Mort's a big man in these parts, miss. No one's going to call him out unless they've got a mountain of proof Mort's not what he seems."

"Suppose," Grace said slowly, turning to face Sheriff Smith, "I gave you that proof. What would you do with it?"

Ray, watching the girl's lovely face, sensed the caution behind her words. Before Perry could frame a reply to Grace's question, Ray cut in.

"You don't have to be careful what you say to the sheriff, Grace. He's not Salter's man."

"If I'd thought that," she retorted, "I wouldn't be

here, Ray. What I'm afraid of is that he might say something or do something that would make Salter suspicious and. . . ."

"And Mort'd go after your pa?"

Grace nodded.

"He can go away for a while," Ray suggested, but the tall girl wagged her head negatively.

"You don't know my father. He wouldn't run from anything."

Perry squared up in the chair. "If you give me something solid," he said to Grace, "I'll run it down, Miss Fenwick, and Mort won't know anything's going on until I come down on him. Either that, or, if it proves invalid information, I'll never say a word about it to Mort or anyone else."

They waited. Beyond the combination office and jail Welton was stirring around them as the heat lessened and evening approached. Sheriff Smith's impatience prompted him to say—"Well?"—but Grace was not yet resolved. Even Ray's urgings brought no response from her. Both men could understand her predicament, but being men could not plumb its depths.

Ray was making a cigarette. Perry Smith was studying his hands and frowning when Grace finally faced them.

"All right," she said, but there was fear in her face and she pushed the words out rapidly, making them run together. "He'll kill my father if he finds out what I know. What I'm going to tell you. He'll kill me, too."

The sheriff ceased regarding his hands. "It takes two to make a killing," he said, "and all Mort's riders and even his two gunmen got to know, first, that someone's got to be killed, Miss Fenwick. Unless they know that they got no reason to kill anyone.

That's part of my job . . . to see to it that folks don't get killed. I've had lots of experience at it, too, so go ahead and speak out and leave that killin' business up to me."

"Duncan Holt," the handsome girl said, her voice roughening with apprehension, "knows the mountain ranges better than anyone." She raised her eyes to Ray. "Excepting you, possibly . . . at least Joe Mitchell told me you knew them better."

"Go on," Perry growled impatiently.

"He brings Salter's men into the mountains, rounds up unmarked cattle, and drives them to Mexico!"

Chapter Nine

Instead of looking surprised at Grace's allegation Perry Smith returned to studying his hands. But now he was solemnly frowning down at them.

"Any proof of that?" he asked eventually.

"Yes, I have proof, Sheriff, but better than that I can lead you to the mountain meadows and you can see Duncan do it yourself."

This brought the sheriffs head up. "How do you know he'll show up, miss?" he asked quickly, doubt and suspicion visible in his gaze.

"Because, as Ray told you, I ride out a lot. I've sat back in the trees watching Duncan's men work the herds. They follow a routine of checking for unmarked animals, cutting them out, holding, them bunched until they have a herd, then driving them easterly through the mountains until they're above Salter's ranch, then down across his land where they can't be tracked . . . then keep on going south."

"All right," Ray said, "that explains how they do it, Grace, but like the sheriff asked . . . how do you know *when* they'll do it?"

"I'm not absolutely certain," the girl answered, "but they also follow a pattern here. They wait until the upland ranchers have finished working a herd, then they move in. I think they do it that way because they know the mountain cowmen will have no reason to go back and work the same herd again until next year." Grace paused, switched her gaze from Ray to Perry Smith. "They're due to hit Joe Mitchell within a week."

"You mean Joe's worked his critters?" Smith asked.

Grace nodded. "Yes, my father took the men up into the meadows today. That's why I decided to ride down here. No one will know I'm not at the ranch."

"I wouldn't bet on that," Ray said dryly. "Seems to me Mort's got spies all through the mountains." Grace's head swung quickly and Ray, reading the antagonism in her expression, added quickly: "Not your father, now. I'm not naming names at all, Grace."

Sheriff Smith got up, walked once across the office and back, and stopped with his back to Grace, facing Ray's cell. "You knew something about this?" he queried.

"About this," Ray answered, "no. But I can tell you that Duncan takes those cattle into Mexico and either sells them outright or trades them for nearly as many Mex critters which he brings back to Salter's range."

The sheriff rummaged in a shirt pocket for his tobacco sack. As he worked up a quirly, Ray regarded Grace. The long-legged girl was watching Perry light up and exhale. Feeling Ray's stare, she turned a little, exchanged a long glance with him, began to color, and turned away.

"I always wondered," the lawman said, "how Mort built up his herds so fast. 'Course, he's got money. But the rub comes in, leastways to me, like this. Mort never seemed to lose cattle like other folks did." Smith scratched his nose, then blew out a big breath. He considered Ray through the bars briefly, then began pacing. "If that whelp really did railroad you, Ray. . . ." He slammed out the cigarette and tugged his hat forward. "All right," he barked, facing Grace. "You go on home. I'll ride up there tonight maybe."

She cut him off. "You can't leave Ray here! Mort will hear that he's here. He'll send men in to. . . ."

"Like I said," the sheriff growled impatiently, cutting her off, "my job involves savin' lives as well as snuffin' one out every now and then. You just go on home and leave Ray to me."

She hesitated, staring at Ray. He nodded at her. "Do like he says."

"I could leave you my gun."

Before Ray could speak, Perry exclaimed: "He don't need your gun, ma'am! He's got one of his own. Now go on home." As the girl started toward the door, the sheriff spoke again. "On second thought maybe we'd better meet somewhere, ma'am. Might look odd, me ridin' up there right now."

"You just stick to the trail," Grace said, holding the door latch. "I'll find you."

After she was gone, Perry bent a skeptical glance toward Ray. "If she's right, Mort Salter's in trouble. If she's wrong . . . or if this is something you two worked up between you. . . ."

"Perry, you're the most suspicious man I've ever known. How could I work up anything with her?"

Smith retrieved Ray's gun from his desk before answering. In fact, not until he was unlocking the cell door did he say: "Ray, I may not be the brightest feller alive but there's sure nothing wrong with my eyesight. I saw how that girl looked at you when she didn't think either of us was watchin' her."

Ray accepted the gun but stood stockstill inside

the cell. Sheriff Smith started forward, then looked back and stopped, impatience in his expression.

"Well, have you taken root or something? Come on, you're going with me. If she's right, I'll apologize. If it's some kind of trick, you'll still be close by."

"Perry, that girl hates my guts."

"Maybe," Smith said philosophically, narrowing his eyes at the younger man. "But if I had a silver-mounted saddle and was a gamblin' man, I sure wouldn't bet it on that with any expectations of winning. Now come on, will you?"

They rode out of Welton side-by-side and traveling westerly to avoid using the main north-south roadway where their departure would be certain to arouse quick and indignant comment. Well away from town and with shadows engulfing them, they beat a steady route northerly toward the foothills. After a time the sheriff, who had been thoughtfully silent, said: "Duncan might not hit Joe's cattle for days. I don't cherish the idea of lyin' out in those doggoned hills livin' on jerky and spring water until he does, either."

"You could just let him run the cattle off," Ray said.

Perry muttered a dour oath. "You know better'n that. I got a job to do and I'll do it."

"Like the time you ambushed me?"

Smith's face darkened. For another half mile he made no additional comment, then, drawing up in the saddle to throw a hard glance toward the foothills, he said: "Ray, if Salter really did railroad you and made me a part of it . . . he better sprout wings because I'm a mite sensitive about bein' used like that."

They hit the first rise with darkness coming down to meet them. It was not difficult to keep to the trail although the moonless sky conspired with the gloomy forest to make progress more a matter of knowing the way instinctively than being able to see it.

"Sure dark," the sheriff said, as they left the trees and cut into Mitchell Meadow.

"There won't be a moon for another three days, either," Ray told him.

Smith looked around. "How do you know that?"

Ray shrugged. "Part of my plan," he said. "Hit him in the dark, Perry."

The sheriffs head whipped forward. He drew down holding up his hand for stillness. "Someone's coming."

"Not coming . . . following. It's Grace."

Perry twisted in the saddle, watching the girl take shape and substance. "You knew she was back there?"

"I only suspected it," replied Ray. "Can't hear anything when you're riding over pine needles. I figured she'd meet us long before we got up where some of Joe's hands might sight us."

Grace was riding a dark chestnut horse that glistened darkly. He was a stocking-legged animal with a flaxen mane and tail. She walked him up close, then drew back. Instead of greeting either man, she said: "I had to tell Joe."

Sheriff Smith said something under his breath. "Why did you have to?" he demanded in a sharp tone. "I don't put too much faith in Joe and never have."

"Because," Grace flared at him, "two of his riders quit and he hired two new ones."

"Well, what the devil has that . . . ?"

"Sheriff," the girl said fiercely, "if you don't want

my help, just say so. Otherwise, shut up until I'm finished!"

Ray peered at Perry from under his hat brim. The sheriffs mouth was drawn out thinly and his angry eyes sparked. He swallowed with visible effort, then said: "Excuse me. Go on, ma'am."

"The two new men Joe hired are Salter's riders. I know they are. I've seen them both in the mountains with Duncan Holt."

Ray pursed his lips and blew out a silent whistle over the implications here. Even the sheriff's expression changed; he began nodding his head up and down in small, choppy motions.

"That'll make it real handy for Duncan, won't it?" he growled. "Two hands to. . . ." He broke off to study the girl. "Did you tell that to Joe?"

"Yes, I had to figure some way to get us help."

"We don't need any help," Smith said sharply.

"That's where you're wrong, Sheriff. You're going to need all the help you can get, because as soon as you jump Duncan, he's going to have to kill you both for what you know."

"Neither Ray Kelly nor I came down in the last rain," Smith said dryly. "We can look after ourselves with Duncan Holt."

"Not with Salter's men behind you, too, you can't," Grace retorted. "And that's what will be behind you if there is any shooting, Sheriff. Gunshots carry a long way in these mountains. If Salter's two gun hands are behind you and Duncan is in front. . . ." Grace let the words trail off into silence.

After a moment Ray said: "What can Joe do?"

"He's going to start a continuous poker game to-night and keep it going."

The sheriff scowled. "A poker game?" he said.

"Yes. Salter's two men will sit in. Joe will see to that. Then, if there's any trouble, Joe will use his gun to keep them at the ranch."

Smith considered this with a screwed-up face. He said: "Ma'am, if you've got this figured out right, you don't think we've got much of a chance."

"I'll tell you what I think," Grace told him bluntly. "I think you have no idea how deadly Duncan Holt and Mort Salter will be if anyone shows them up as big-time rustlers."

Ray had been watching her, saying nothing, but now in a quiet way he said: "Grace, what will your father's position be in this? Salter had the bank put him up here as Joe's foreman. You knew that, didn't you?"

"Yes, I knew that. I also know why Salter did that. Because he knows my father is absolutely honest, Ray, and will not permit Mitchell's riders to ride with a long loop. In other words, Salter knew my father would not let the cowboys roam the hills like Joe used to let them do, and this gave Salter's hands a free run of the high country ranges."

"He used your pa, too?" Sheriff Smith asked, then answered himself when the girl kept silent. "That ought to make me feel better, but it don't." He regarded the girl gravely. "Does Duncan ever hit the herds at night?"

"No, Sheriff, but you'd never get up in here in broad daylight without being seen." She reined around. "Follow me," she ordered. "Stay close because it'll be dark."

As they rode upward across the meadow toward the higher, forested headlands, Perry Smith twisted and threw a look of discomfort and helplessness at

Ray. The younger man laughed silently back at him, then they both concentrated on riding.

Grace proved to Ray's satisfaction that she knew the uplands nearly as well as he did himself. She switched from cattle trails to buck runs without hesitation, seemingly knowing exactly where she would find each. And she kept steadily northeasterly toward the big, grassy meadows which, in winter, were deeply covered with snow, but which during summer remained green into late September, watered by snow run-off.

They passed from forest to glen and back into forest again. Several times they heard the startled *thump* of bedded deer springing up at their approach to go crashing off into the night, and they rode through equally as surprised but less agile bunches of JM cattle.

Topping out near ten o'clock along a thin and treeless ridge, they could make out a huge mountain meadow directly below them. It was faintly dotted with many dark cow shapes, a few grazing but mostly lying bulkily, shapelessly, low in the grass.

"That's where the crew worked today," Grace told them. "They bunched up everything they located in this area." She motioned outward with one hand. "It's a sizable herd," she said, and dropped the hand, looking around past Sheriff Smith to Ray. "If they operate as I've seen them do before, they'll probably ride up in here about daybreak." She paused, glanced at Perry briefly, then back to Ray again. "You'll have to be very careful."

"We will be," the younger man told her. "Now you'd better head back."

But she did not move. "Sheriff? I could go back to Welton and get a posse for you."

But Perry's flinty stare was ranging easterly where Salter's men must come up to enter the meadow. "Who needs a posse?" he said disinterestedly, studying the landfalls. "How many men will Duncan have?"

"No less than ten, Sheriff."

"Well, that's about right," Smith said, finally throwing a look at Ray. "Five to one, that's about the right odds for cattle thieves, isn't it?"

Ray did not answer. He urged his horse forward, groped in the darkness for Grace's fingers, found them, and closed his fist around them. "Better head back now," he said very quietly. "And Grace . . . ?"

"Yes."

"Much obliged."

"You don't owe me anything," she said, making no move to free her hand.

"Well," he said frankly, "I had something else in mind to trip Salter up . . . but this will be a lot better and quicker, so I kind of think I do owe you something."

She did not lower her eyes as she raised the reins preparatory to turning back. Nor did she speak again, but for the fleetingest second she returned the hard pressure of Ray's fingers, then she drew her hand away quickly, and passed beyond sight back down the way they had come.

Without looking around, the sheriff said: "Nope, if I had me a real fine silver-mounted saddle and wanted to bet it on something . . . you 'n' that girl'd be the last thing I'd wager it on. I mean about her hatin' your guts, Ray."

Ray dismounted with his horse between them. As he worked the cinch loose, he muttered: "If there's one thing I could never abide, it is lawmen with eyes in the backs of their heads."

Sheriff Smith said no more. He watched Ray a moment, then sighed, swung down, drew forth his carbine, loosened his cinch, and sat down. It was not yet midnight; they had a long wait ahead of them.

Chapter Ten

This land of the mountain cowmen was a tumbled, upended country of meadows and forest with always the black-cut higher peaks standing darkly against the skyline. It was a cool country in summer and a frigid land in winter, but most significantly to Ray Kelly, who knew it well, it was a vast country where men could hide indefinitely with small fear of encountering others. He knew that if Duncan Holt's riders became suspicious and faded into the forest, Sheriff Smith's chance of capturing even one of them would be remote indeed, and it was his hope that at least one of the rustling crew might be apprehended.

He remarked on this to the lawman and Smith, with little more than a cursory knowledge of the high country, suggested that Ray take them to some site where he thought a capture might be effected. They accordingly trailed along the treeless ridge where Grace had left them, to a dusty cattle trail, descended it, struck the meadow where its forested fringe came down to the grass, rode northeasterly as far as a snow-fed tumbling creek, and there resumed their vigil upon enough of a rise to be able to see down across the meadow to the grazing cattle against the sharply standing bluffs to the south.

Neither man said much and for Ray Kelly at least the waning night was a time for hard reflection and ultimately gentle thoughts of George Fenwick's daughter. He had not, at first, been particularly drawn to her. But he had never been a woman's man in any case and their meetings had, until this night, been anything but conducive to romance. His picture of her now was different. Why it was he could not explain even to himself. Surely the fleeting pressure of her fingers upon his hand was nothing to build upon, yet, with nothing else actually, he did build upon it.

Tall and shapely with a manner to her that struck through a man, he remembered her direct and steady way of looking at a person, recalled, too, her full, composed lips and the strong sweep of her stride. Remembered how the sun had struck against her coppery hair, and dwelt for a time on her long silences, knowing somehow that in a woman silence could mean many things and wondering now, in her case, what it meant where he was concerned.

There was the stuff of dreams in his mind, and after the fashion of introspective men he did not check his imaginings now. Not until, shortly before dawn, Perry Smith growled deeply in his throat that a horse was coming.

They straightened up off the pine needles, turned suddenly alert and wary. The horse carried a rider but they knew this only from the way the animal approached, briskly, undeviatingly, in a purposeful manner until the paling sky backgrounded a solitary horseman emerging onto the meadow from the north.

"Scout," Perry said softly. "Come along some easterly trail keepin' a look-out."

Ray said nothing. He watched the cowboy draw up and sit motionlessly, gazing slowly around the meadow. He knew the man was satisfied when he made a cigarette and lit it, making no attempt to conceal the match flame. It occurred to him there might be other riders coming along through the trees bearing on westward and he got carefully to his feet beckoning to the sheriff. When they were back by their horses, Ray made a motion with his hand as though to pinch off his mount's wind.

"In case any others come along and get close enough for our critters to smell 'em and whinny," he explained.

The sheriff understood and nodded, moving closer to his horse.

It was a long wait, though. They could tell that it was going to be by the way the unidentified rider swung down, squatted in the grass gazing at the cattle, thumbed back his hat, and drowsed.

"Duncan's pretty careful," the sheriff growled. "You'd think with things goin' so well he wouldn't go to all the trouble."

Thinking back to shared campfires when he and Duncan Holt had been together, Ray recalled that JM's ex-foreman had always been a deliberate man. It pained him now, thinking back to shared confidences, to times of pleasure and laughter together, to realize how much time had passed, so much that he stood there now, gun in hand, waiting to catch or kill Duncan Holt.

Sheriff Smith must have caught some of this, for he said faintly: "Ray, if you want to stay out of sight and keep the others off my back with your carbine, I'll go. . . ."

"No, Perry. What used to be is gone." He did not enlarge upon this and exerted an inner effort to turn his mind away from the past. "Do you recognize that man?"

Smith said he did not.

Time passed slowly. The sky was brightening faintly off in the east, showing snag-toothed peaks and breaks. Around them cattle were stirring, arising to move off leisurely in search of graze. Perry's voice came again as low and quiet as before.

"I reckon he's in no hurry," he opined, referring to Duncan Holt. "Can't drive cattle through a forest in the dark anyway."

When Smith's final word died away, Ray saw the hunkering cowboy rise up, face easterly, and cock his head in an attitude of strong listening. He stood thus for only a moment, then stepped across his mount and reined slowly toward the forest. He had not quite reached it when a blur of dark shapes emerged, engulfed him, and stopped.

"She wasn't wrong," Perry said, meaning Grace Fenwick. "There's at least ten of them."

Ray wiped sweat off his palm along the seam of his trousers without taking his eyes off the strangers. "Do you make any of them out?" he asked.

Smith did not answer right away, not until the riders were splitting up, moving off, angling as though to ride completely around the meadow, then, as Ray thought, to begin their gradual drive northward or eastward, pushing the cattle toward the forest and some trail beyond, out of sight in the trees. He began to straighten up. Two of the moving silhouettes were coming toward the place where he and Perry waited. Then the sheriff spoke, replying to Ray's earlier question.

"Yeah, Ray, I recognize two of 'em. The ones ridin' toward us. That feller on the left, on the meadow side, is Duncan. The other feller is. . . ."

"I know him," Ray said shortly. "He must be one

of the riders who quit JM yesterday. His name's Carter Wilson." Ray swore with bitter feeling. "He saved my bacon, Perry. It was him warned me about Fenwick's sending Salter word I was at JM."

Smith hesitated briefly, then edged forward. "Can't expect a feller to trade shots with folks he owes favors to," he said gruffly. "I'll handle this."

Ray watched the riders curve along side-by-side, bending southwesterly with the forest's contour. "Hell," he exclaimed. "When I was at Yuma, I looked forward to runnin' down Mort's men but this. . . ."

"I understand, kid. Now we'd better shut up."

The horsemen were close enough to hear voices. They rode loosely as men do that have no reasons for apprehension, and it was this very fact that permitted Perry Smith to stop them, turn them suddenly silent and staring with astonishment when he stepped out of the trees, barred their way with his cocked carbine, and said: "Not a sound, boys. Not one peep out of either of you."

It was a bad moment and Ray, perhaps better than Perry Smith, knew how bad it was. He knew Duncan Holt too well to believe the ex-foreman would submit tamely to arrest. He looked up, watched Duncan's familiar, dark, and hawkish face blank over with craftiness, with hard and wrathful defiance, and stepped into view off to one side, cocking his own carbine so that the sound carried easily to the motionless mounted men.

"Dunc, don't be a fool."

The dark man turned slowly, looking down. "You," he breathed.

"Yeah, me. Perry, go ahead and disarm 'em." As Smith started forward, Duncan Holt's gaze swung to bear flintily on him. Ray spoke again softly. "Five years is a long time, Dunc. A feller gets a little bitter thinking about what put him away. He gets to believe killin' the man responsible or those who work for him could be a real pleasure. Don't make a move or I'll prove to you how that is."

Duncan did not move; he clearly believed Ray would kill him, but the darkness of his natural coloring grew steadily blacker with anger. When Perry had disarmed both men, Holt said: "What the hell do you two idiots think you're doing anyway?"

Smith spat aside then looked up. "Capturin' us a nice brace of cow thieves."

"Cow thieves," Holt snorted. "What've we stolen?"

Perry turned saturnine. "Save it," he growled. "Bluster might work in a law court but not up here." He switched his attention to Carter Wilson. "Did you quit JM yesterday?" he asked.

Wilson nodded without speaking. Ray grounded the carbine and leaned upon it. "Duncan here tell you to, Wilson?"

The cowboy looked over at Holt, still saying nothing. Duncan, studying Ray Kelly, made a slow, mirthless smile. "Kid," he said evenly, "you're sure on the wrong side this time."

Ray gestured. "Get down and lead your horses back into the trees." As the prisoners were obeying, he went closer to Salter's range boss. "Dunc, I was on the wrong side last time, too . . . but I was loyal."

"And you got five years for it," Holt snarled, moving off under Perry Smith's cocked carbine.

"But I can sleep nights," Ray said shortly. "Can you?"

They halted well back out of sight in the trees. Smith bound each prisoner's hands behind him, used their belts to secure their ankles, then pushed them down upon the ground in a sitting position.

"Think we ought to gag 'em?" he asked.

Ray shook his head, squatting behind Salter's men. "Naw, they're too smart to yell, Perry. Wouldn't either of them want to get their skull split."

Dawn was nearing now; the sky was a very delicate pastel blue, almost blue steel gray. It was bright enough for the men, hunkering in the trees, to observe how Duncan's rustlers worked. They did not lift their mounts out of a walk nor in any other way agitate the cattle. They simply closed around the meadow, riding inward pincer-like, drifting the cattle northward and bunching them from the wings as they moved. It was, Ray thought, a very professional job; men without a lot of experience would not be so wise in this quiet and efficient method of stealing a large herd of animals. He leaned forward behind Duncan Holt.

"Still want to know whose cattle you've stolen, Dunc?"

"Go to hell!"

Ray settled back. For a while no one said anything, then Ray brushed Perry Smith's arm. "We'd better head out," he suggested. "We've seen enough anyway and those fellers are going to begin wondering where Dunc and Carter are pretty quick now."

They boosted both of Mort Salter's men upon the horses, took the reins of the bound men's animals, and started southwesterly through the trees toward the same steep trail that had permitted them to get down into the meadow. Where the trees ended, there was nothing for it but to move across open country to the trail and start up it. Ray, riding twisted in the saddle, kept a long look on Holt's distant crew of riders. The cowboys appeared intent upon getting their stolen herd headed easterly in the right direction. They had not discovered the loss of two of their companions.

They did not discover it, in fact, until Holt, Wilson, and their captors were well down the far side of the trail heading for the Welton plains and making a wide circuit to avoid Mitchell Meadows.

Coming at last to open country, Ray drew Duncan Holt's animal up beside him, made a cigarette, stuck it between the rustler's lips, and lit it. They rode silently for several miles with flashing early sunlight making their world brilliantly clear and clean-looking.

"Why, Dunc?" Ray asked finally.

Holt, deep in thought for so long, roused himself to spit out one word. "Money!"

"Did he pay you a lot?"

"Plenty. A percentage, kid."

Silence settled between them again until Welton was in sight and Ray let off a long sigh. "Figured we might meet a reception committee of Salter's men before this," he said. The dark man at his side grunted.

"You know how many rounds there are in a box fight, Ray?"

"Sure."

"Well, because a feller wins one round sure don't make him no champion. Like I said back at the meadow . . . you're on the wrong side again."

Ray turned. Holt's dour expression heightened

the darkly dangerous and hawk-like look of his face. "Something I heard once a long time back," he said musingly. "You think you know a man because you're close to him for a long time, but you never really do, Dunc. I'd have bet my last cartwheel you'd never sell out to Mort Salter an' join Salter's pack against Joe."

"Joe's old," Holt answered coldly. "He's done for. Salter's on the way up. In this life, kid, a man's got to look out for his own best interests first." He threw Ray a hard look. "You're going to find that out right soon now. You've crossed the wrong man in Mort Salter. He'll bust you into a thousand pieces for what you 'n' Perry did tonight."

They rode through Welton at a walk and the few people who were abroad stopped to gape. At the jail, Sheriff Smith got stiffly down and jerked his head sideways without speaking. Beneath the overhang in front of his office where shadows dripped darkly, the door opened and three men loomed bulkily in the opening, obviously having emerged from the sheriffs little building after a long wait. At first neither Perry Smith nor Ray Kelly saw them, but a sharply indrawn breath brought them both around in a flash.

"Hello, Mort," Duncan Holt said flatly. "How'd you get here so fast?"

The shorter, better-dressed of the three men took several steps forward to squint outward. He was clearly startled to see who the prisoners were. But Mort Salter was not a man who could be long kept off balance by surprise.

"I didn't know about this," he said to Holt, and switched a hating stare at Ray Kelly. "I come to swear out a warrant against *him!*"

Perry flagged with his drawn pistol, ignoring Salter and his gunmen. "Inside," he ordered the prisoners. "You other fellers in the doorway there . . . stand clear!"

Chapter Eleven

No one in the Welton country actually knew much about Morton Salter beyond the fact that he had grown both rich and powerful since coming into the Southwest some ten years earlier, but everyone knew him by this time as a dangerous, dictatorial, devious man who had little fear in him and whose ambition rode him pitilessly night and day.

He was in most ways unlike most Westerners. He very rarely wore a gun, and, although he had, during his early years at least, been compelled to ride a horse, he had never learned to ride well and now, rich enough to hire his riding done, he went everywhere by buggy.

He was a short, heavy man with a face blasted out of an environment that had left its marks; his stare was chillingly black and his lipless mouth had a downward droop at the corners. No one knew exactly what Morton Salter's motivation was in amassing wealth, but there were rumors he aspired to the governorship.

Now, standing stiffly in Perry Smith's office, breathing heavily and watching the sheriff lock two of his men in separate cells, the fierce depth of his temper filled the little room suffocatingly.

Off to one side, more wary of the two slouching men behind Salter who were obviously gunfighters than of Mort himself, Ray leaned upon the wall, waiting for the explosion he knew was coming.

Sheriff Smith crossed to his desk, avoided Salter's glittering stare, and tossed a ring of keys upon the desk. Then he turned, drew himself up, and leaned into that fiery look.

"Too bad you came along right now," Smith said, looking steadily down into the shorter man's face. "I wanted to question those two before I visited you, Mort."

"Did you, Sheriff?" Salter ground out in icy tones. "And what did you reckon they'd tell you about me?"

"They work for you, don't they?"

"Lots of saddle bums work for me."

"Uhn-huh. Well, those two were stealin' JM cattle when we took 'em."

Salter continued to glower. "What's that prove?" he spat out. "What my men do after the end of the work day is their business . . . not mine."

"You tellin' me Duncan and that Wilson feller were stealin' those cattle without you knowing anything about it?"

"I'm telling you nothing, Smith. Nothing at all. But I'll give you some advice. Turn Wilson and Holt loose or you'll wish you'd never been born. And lock up that jailbird over there against the wall!"

Smith continued calmly in the face of Salter's deadly glare: "Funny thing about that," he said. "I was sort of thinkin' about deputizing Ray."

Salter's nostrils quivered. For a moment he said nothing, and then he drawled in a tone of voice so strong with menace no one could have missed it: "Smith, you do that. You deputize Kelly . . . because by this time tomorrow night he'll be dead!"

Smith's voice grew an edge to it now. "Mort, you just threatened a man who's goin' to be servin' the law by this time tomorrow night. You kill a lawman and, believe me, there won't be a place in this country you can hide out in."

Salter's color deepened but he seemed suddenly less furious; he even forced a savage smile. "Smith, there won't be but maybe one witness to what I just said. Kelly'll be dead, Holt and Wilson will be out of here, and these two"—Salter jerked his head to indicate the silent, watching gunfighters—"they work for me, too. If you survive, it'll be your word against the five of us." Salter's stare swung across the room to settle triumphantly upon Ray. "I rode in here to swear out a warrant for this man's arrest," he continued, "and I been sittin' here for most o' the night, waiting for you to make it out and enforce it." He returned his gaze to the sheriff's face. "Now let's get it written out and enforced."

"What charge?"

"Cow stealin' for a starter, then attempted assassination and shootin' one of my men in my own ranch yard."

"You got proof, Mort?"

"Would I be here without it?" Salter demanded, and motioned toward the slouching gunfighters. "These two seen Kelly shoot that man at the ranch." He gestured toward Duncan Holt's cell. "Dunc there saw him stampede a herd of mine down near the border . . . him and five of his friends."

"How about the attempted assassination?"

Salter bobbed his head. "That, too; but I didn't bring those boys in with me. Two of 'em that time . . . Kelly and one other. Each of them took a shot at me."

Perry Smith's cloudy gaze drifted to the gunmen.

"Outside," he snapped at them, jerking his head toward the door. "If I want you, I'll call you. Wait outside."

The gunmen looked at Mort Salter for instructions without moving. Ray, watching this interlude, breathed shallowly. If trouble was coming, now was the time for it. He straightened up very gently against the wall.

Salter squinted suspiciously at Smith. "What do you want them to leave for?"

The sheriff's mouth drew down as he replied. "There'll be no shootin' with them outside, Mort. I can't write up a warrant and watch them, too."

Salter considered this, then turned and made a curt motion with one hand. The two silent gunfighters stalked out, and closed the door. Salter kept his eyes on the lawman's face, waiting. Smith sagged into a chair, made a cigarette with considerable deliberation, lit it, exhaled, and gazed up into the cowman's face.

"Mort," he said levelly, "you're a liar!"

Salter went stiff, his mouth slowly closed down, and his jaw muscles bulged. Smith went on talking in the same thin tone of voice.

"In the first place, Duncan didn't see no five riders. In the second place your so-called witnesses didn't see any two men take potshots at you. In the third place. . . ."

Ray's voice came quietly forward, cutting across the sheriffs words, interrupting: "In the third place, Salter, that night in your yard it was black as the ace of spades. It was also moonless the night your herd got hit down near the border. No one saw anything. They couldn't have seen anything. It was too dark. But if you want to try and make those charges stick in court . . . this time I'm ready for you. I've got witnesses, too. Every man in the Welton country can swear it was too dark the night your man was shot and the night your herd was hit to identify anyone!"

Salter remained like stone for a long time, then he turned slightly, facing toward Duncan Holt's cell. Beyond the bars, holding to them with both hands, Holt was staring sideways at Ray.

"Well?" Salter demanded of the prisoner. "You saw five of 'em didn't you, Dunc?"

Holt shuffled his feet without immediately replying. He turned slowly to gaze steadily out at Salter. It was obvious from his expression he wished to say something privately to Salter. All he did finally say was: "Got to be careful here, Mort."

"Careful!" Salter exploded. "Careful of what? These two tomfools! You saw Kelly and his friends. You're goin' to swear to that in court!"

Perry Smith pushed up out of the chair. "Mort," he intoned quietly, "I think you'd best forget that warrant and get along home. You see, there wasn't any five riders. There never has been. I don't know where you got that information, but it's plumb wrong."

"You know that for a fact, do you!" exclaimed Salter, facing the sheriff fiercely.

Smith nodded. "For a fact," he said.

Ray saw Salter's eyes narrow, his expression change subtly, and knew Salter had figured out how he had been tricked by Joe Mitchell's tale of Ray's five friends. He was thinking that Joe had to be warned at once, when Salter spoke again.

"And you are refusing to make out that warrant?" he said to Perry Smith.

The sheriff made the faintest of frowns. "Not exactly refusing," he said carefully, choosing his words.

"Just sort of holdin' off until I get more proof Ray ought to be arrested." A thought struck him, and he nodded toward the cell-block. "I want to talk to these two before I do much about Kelly, anyway."

It worked. Salter's mind swung swiftly to this vulnerable spot. He shot a venomous look at Holt and Carter. "You boys tell him nothing," he commanded. "I'll have a lawyer up here from Yuma by day after tomorrow and get you out." Salter crossed toward the door, and paused with his hand on the latch. "Smith, next week Welton'll have a new sheriff. Either that or you'll start using your head."

"What's that supposed to mean, Mort?" Perry asked, knowing well enough what Salter was implying.

"It means no one bucks me, Smith, and goes on livin' in this country. Least of all a two-bit cow-town lawman!"

Salter slammed the door so hard the front wall shook when he left. Ray took two swift steps to cross toward the desk.

"He'll send someone to JM, Perry."

"Why? He doesn't know about the girl."

"Because I got Joe to spread that tale about me having friends ridin' with me. Salter's figured out how I used Joe to trick him."

"Boy," the lawman said, moving swiftly for the first time in days, "you'd better make tracks up there to warn Joe." He rummaged impatiently through a desk drawer, located what he sought, and threw it across to Ray. "Pin that on or stick it in your pocket," he said. "You're a deputy sheriff now."

Ray held the little star briefly in his palm, gazing at it. This, he thought, was anything but what he had imagined his return to Welton might result in.

"Go on, dog-gone it," Sheriff Smith ordered. "And be mighty careful. Mort'll be out there somewhere, waiting. I'll give you odds on it." He shot a sour look at Holt and Carter. "I wish I felt sure someone wouldn't turn these two loose if I went with you."

Beyond Sheriff Smith's office the town was stirring with an excitement that was nebulous but nonetheless real. People watched Ray lope northward on the ugly buckskin and speculated. A few sauntered down toward the sheriff's office with no clear intentions but driven along by increasing curiosity. Nearly everyone had heard of Duncan Holt's capture and Mort Salter's thundering departure from town. There was, saloon talk had it, something pretty big afoot.

The sheriff admitted only one person to his office, Elijah Herman, proprietor of Welton's only dry goods emporium. Elijah was a member of the town council; Smith could not very well exclude him. But he was tired, too, and Elijah's questions drew only short answers.

The thing uppermost in Perry Smith's mind now was the imminent peril Ray was riding into. Even when Councilman Herman urged him to round up a posse and ride out, saying he would personally recruit other townsmen to guard the prisoners, Smith did not hear him the first time.

When Herman persisted, though, Perry came swiftly to a conclusion. Even if Salter's gunmen did get Holt and Carter, they were not as important as Ray. "All right," he agreed finally, snatching up his hat. "You mind the store here, Elijah, and mind it good because those two are going to be mighty important when we bring Mort Salter in for rustling."

He heard Elijah say something but could not distinguish what it was because he was passing through the doorway when the merchant said it. "Hey," he bellowed at the milling men beyond in the doorway. "I need a posse! Go fetch your guns an' horses!"

Chapter Twelve

Ray kept a sharp watch as soon as he had cleared Welton. It seemed improbable to him, as it had to Perry Smith, that Salter would concentrate all his attention upon Joe Mitchell. Salter had left absolutely no doubt whatsoever that his hatred of Ray Kelly was an all-consuming emotion. Riding easterly instead of northerly, he weighed his chances, considered the situation before him, and made a careful balance. This was an affair in which he would be allowed no margin of error; his first mistake would be his last one.

Reckoning on Salter's leaving gunmen athwart the known routes into the uplands, he deliberately rode the full distance to Salter's own range. He wasted time doing this and knew it, was agitated by this knowledge, but it would in his opinion be better to arrive late at JM than not to arrive there at all, which he felt sure would be the case if he loped recklessly into the mountains via the established trails. Furthermore, while there would from now on be no safe place in the night for him, he would be least expected to show up at Salter's ranch.

This premise at least was sound; he cut across Salter's bedding ground without seeing anything except cattle. Afterward, he made for the forested corridor from which he had shot at Salter. Beyond that site he remembered the trail reasonably well, but it was slow going in the dark.

Unexpectedly he cut the trail of Joe Mitchell's rustled herd and this was a fortuitous thing; here were broken branches, trampled pine needles, and a dim but discernibly broad pathway leading around under the high peaks. Here, too, he rode faster, knowing that even if Salter had a man or two up in here, they would hesitate to fire on anyone coming from the direction of their home ranch, particularly in the forest's gloom, night-heightened so that recognition would be nearly impossible.

The tree scatter thinned a little before Ray came within sight of the meadow from which Duncan Holt had stolen Joe Mitchell's herd. He did not slow until at the very edge, when he needed a moment to make certain no Salter men were beyond in the open country. Afterward, he rode carefully forward, cut southerly over the meadow, and did not relax until he was back into the forest on the meadow's lower side. It was, he thought, very reassuring even to a man who had spent most of his life on the plains to have the darkness and the forest around him.

It was a goodly ride from the upper, large meadow to JM and he fretted because caution forbade traveling fast. He could not approximate the time very well because the shades of night varied greatly.

Coming finally to within sight of Mitchell Meadow, he dismounted and went warily forward on foot. Having angled southeasterly for the past hour, he found himself where he expected, within hailing distance of Joe Mitchell's house. It was not difficult, here, to estimate the distance because nearly every window in Mitchell's low log residence shone with bright lamplight.

Leaving the buckskin tied beyond sight from the yard, he crept forward, carbine in hand. He felt a growing fear, having expected to hear gunshots; he found this heavy silence much worse. Yellowish light touched along the saddled backs of a number of horses tied in front of Mitchell's house. Two lounging figures near the animals, one smoking, were clearly Salter's outside guards.

He straightened up, peering ahead. What was Salter doing in there? He surely had known Ray and perhaps the sheriff as well would be showing up at JM before daybreak.

Speculation, though, resolved nothing. Keeping a sidling watch on the guards, he studied the rest of the yard. George Fenwick's house also had a lamp burning, but turned low. The bunkhouse was dark and, except for the guards, the yard was empty. There was something eerie about all this. It never crossed his mind that Mort Salter might have set a trap, not even when he moved softly around through the trees so as to emerge into the yard in such a way as to keep the bunkhouse between himself and the lounging guards—and out of nowhere a man hurled himself upright from a low bent-over crouch, swinging from the hips to catch hold of Ray with his straining arms.

Ray had no time to shoot; he had scarcely time enough to react defensively, then the man was on him. One arm began a high overhand swing. Ray ducked away and the clubbed gun *whooshed* past his face. He dropped the carbine, twisting away and throwing a short jab, but the shadow bore in, and having two advantages, that of surprise and offence, carried Ray jarringly back against a huge old red fir tree seeking to slam his head against the rough trunk. Again Ray anticipated his attacker and rolled sideways, avoiding the bent, groping fingers.

He hit the stranger a short, powerful blow in the

stomach. The man sucked back and bent a little to protect himself. Ray brought a knee up hard before the cowboy could straighten up. There was a meaty sound followed by an expulsion of explosive breath. The man moved back heavily; he was in pain and raised his face to search the near night for Ray's next move. He had not long to wait. Without having the least idea who his attacker was, Ray nonetheless recognized in him a much experienced rough-and-tumble battler. Moreover, he could tell from the man's pressure against him that he was easily fifty pounds heavier. He could not, therefore, confine himself to defense if he hoped to walk away, and, taking full advantage of the stranger's immediate discomfort, he lunged outward, away from the tree, whipped his body sideways, and threw a long, blasting blow that rocked his adversary.

The heavier man, however, did not go down. He gave more ground, though, and covered up as best he could, trading space for time. Ray, resolved to give him no rest, kept stalking him with his knuckles, jarring him constantly backward until the rider's arms dropped and his glazed eyes, scarcely seen in the gloom, blinked stupidly, half consciously. Then he halted, drawing heavily for wind, waiting for his adversary's eyes to clear.

It was a long, still moment full of unnaturalness, and, when Ray saw the big man's face regain its color, he said: "Had enough?"

Instead of conceding, the big man dug his toes in and catapulted forward, bearing Ray to the ground, staking his chances on this desperate maneuver, striking at Ray's face with his fists, clawing for his eyes, and using his weight to hold the lighter, more vigorous man beneath him. But it was in any case the final act of an injured fighter and Ray threw the man off, whirled upright, and was waiting with a cocked fist. He fired it as the larger man was rising, knocking him backward. He never did collapse, but held himself numbly off the ground, dimly reflexing to protect his vital parts from further injury, reacting instinctively while the memory of other battles came cloudily into his half consciousness.

He was beaten. Ray knew it and pushed him into a sitting position, frisked him for a hide-out gun, found nothing, not even a boot knife, and hunkered forward, facing the stranger while his lungs sucked in powerful lungfuls of the insufficient night air.

"Had enough?" he asked again, and this time the beaten man nodded his head, raised a hand to feel his cut and swelling mouth, and gazed with clearing vision at his vanquisher.

"They'll get you just the same," he mumbled, gazing at the back of one hand. "For a thousand dollars one of 'em'll get you, Kelly."

Ray threw the man a tough look. "They'll get the chance." He got up, winced from an ache in his side, and moved closer, unbuckled the man's shell belt and trouser belt, and growled: "Lie down and roll over on your belly."

The cowboy made no resistance while Ray bound his ankles and arms, and rolled him over, face up, but his eyes were eloquent with malevolence.

"Where is Salter . . . in the house?"

The glittering stare remained unwavering and the man's battered lips did not part.

Ray gazed steadily downward for a moment, then very deliberately knelt beside the man, tore a strip from his shirt, fashioned and applied a gag, then drew a match from his pocket, removed his hat to shield the flame, and lit it. "Your last chance to talk," he said, moving the match forward so that its heat touched the bound man's jaw. "Where is Salter . . . what's he up to?"

The flame speared upward, touching flesh. The bound man jerked his head away, growling beneath the gag. Ray doused the match and pulled away his gag.

"He's in the house, waitin' for you," the cowboy said bitterly. "He's got Joe an' Fenwick and Fenwick's girl in there." The fire-pointed eyes flared. "He's goin' to hang you, Kelly. Hang you slow."

"How many more are out here, hidin'?"

"Couple more. One behind the house to the east. Another feller down at the lower end of the meadow, waitin' for you to come up from the plain."

"That one's harmless," Ray said, referring to the man down near the forest's edge. He got up. The hurt in his side made him flinch a second time. "But I'd better take care of the one behind the house." He started to readjust the gag.

"Wait a second," the cowboy said rapidly. "Listen, you can't leave me lyin' here like this."

"Someone'll find you," Ray said, reaching forward toward the gag again.

"No! Listen, Kelly, if they get you, no one'll know where I am."

"I'm gambling no one'll get me," Ray said dryly.

"Don't be a fool. Mort's got seven men up here. Six not countin' me. He knows cussed well you'll show up here sooner or later and he's waiting. You don't stand a chance."

"Pretty sure of himself, isn't he?"

"He knows you'll try an' help Mitchell. Listen, turn me loose, an' I swear I'll get my horse and slope. I give you my word, Kelly."

Ray pushed the gag roughly into place without answering, made sure it was securely tied, checked the bound man's other fastenings, ignored the choked incoherence coming from behind the gag, and moved off through the forest, heading around toward the rear of Joe Mitchell's house.

It took longer to locate Salter's second hidden guard, but feeling that time was no longer as important as he had formerly considered it, and basing this upon what the beaten man had told him about Salter's using Joe Mitchell and the Fenwicks as hostages, he lingered in the tree shadows for nearly half an hour before catching a dark blur of movement down near the last fringe of forest where a man's broad back moved.

He began inching onward, placing one foot carefully forward and bringing his weight to bear upon it before moving the second foot. It took an indeterminate length of time to stalk close enough to halt and draw his handgun and straighten up with less than ten feet between his pistol barrel and the drowsing sentry, but he accomplished it without a sound.

"Mister, if you so much as open your mouth, you're dead."

The sentinel did not move; he might not have heard Ray's strong whisper at all, he was so still. Ray moved in behind him, took away his pistol, and kicked the carbine that the man had leaned against a tree into the darkness, then ordered the man to face around.

This second rider was also a stranger. They stood in dank gloom, gazing upon one another, and the cowboy seemed neither greatly surprised to find himself captured nor particularly annoyed, either. He even grinned at Ray.

"Funny how folks misjudge people, ain't it?" he said conversationally, studying Ray's features thoughtfully. "Mort said you didn't have sense enough to come in outta the rain. Duncan Holt said you was real good with a gun but pretty much of a kid in everything else." The man's gaze lowered, held briefly to the cocked pistol, then came up again. "Now, me . . . I'd say you wasn't no kid and you wasn't no fool, either, slippin' up on me like that. How'd you find me, Kelly?"

"A friend of yours told me you were over here."

The cowboy's brow wrinkled; the respect in his gaze heightened. "You mean Bull Markly?"

"I don't know his name. He's lying over there in the trees. He was watching for me, too."

"You slipped up on him, too?"

"No, he jumped me and I whipped him."

The cowboy's smile faded and his gaze widened. "You . . . whupped Bull Markly in a fair fight?"

"Not too fair a fight," Ray said dryly. "But he's whipped and hog-tied. Now you turn around and back up close to me."

The range man understood at once and began wagging his head. "You'll have to shoot me," he said. "I got a pretty thin skull an' don't favor bein' knocked over the head."

Ray, feeling no animosity for this man, in fact seeing in him the image of dozens of range men like him who had been his friends and campfire companions in years past, nodded his head. "All right, lie down then, and I'll tie you up."

The rider hesitated only briefly. It was as typical of

him that he expected no treachery as it was of Ray Kelly that he planned none. The man eased down. Ray holstered his gun and secured the sentinel without a word passing between them until he made the gag and was beginning to apply it. Then the rider said: "Kelly, be smart and ride on. Mort's got enough men on your trail to smother you. You can't help Mitchell, either. He's got him hog-tied with mortgages and such like."

"Thanks for the advice," Ray said, tied the gag in place, turned the man upon his back, touched his hat brim in salute, and faded out in the darkness, heading for the rear of Mitchell's house.

Chapter Thirteen

Ray moved out of the trees and halted to keen the night. There was neither sound nor movement. The thin, winey night air would have shown one and brought echoes of the other. His thoughts ran fast now and uncertain. Perhaps the wisest course would be to wait. Perry Smith, he thought, would eventually come up. He even considered, but only very briefly, riding back to Welton for help. But this would use up too much time, and, knowing how Mort Salter thought, he knew the rustler baron would not wait at JM indefinitely. Presently making up his mind, he paced light-footedly forward, coming down near the dark rear wall of Mitchell's log house. By his nearest calculation, if Salter had ridden to JM with six riders and had detached three as hidden sentinels, he could not now be in Joe's house with more than one man because obviously two others were outside with the horses—or had been outside at any rate.

That, he knew, would make no difference. At the first sound of trouble from within the house, those two would immediately burst in. He could there-fore count on odds of four to one. Joe and George Fenwick would be disarmed and helpless to help him, he knew. He was not, for that matter, convinced Fenwick would not join Salter against him. He made a wry grimace—when a man was thinking in terms of four to one odds adding another man did not make any appreciable difference.

He ranged ahead and flattened against the rear of Joe's house, listening. There was nothing to hear; either the people within were silent, or the great logs deadened all sound. He palmed his gun, was edging toward the window he had used once before to gain entrance, when the sharp, hard sound of galloping horses coming on from the west, up and across Mitchell Meadow, turned him to stone.

There had to be no less than ten riders, he judged, dropping low and scuttling to the extreme south corner of the log wall. If it was more of Salter's men, he not only would be unable to help Salter's hostages, he would be in a very bad position himself.

Ahead, softly fluted in the night, came a call: "Hold up there! Hey, draw down, you fellers!"

There was no diminishing of the hoof beats and a muted gunshot blasted the night. This was instantly answered by an angry chorus of returned shots, deep-throated and booming—the sound of handguns replying to a carbine.

From within the house there was a sudden loud yell, the rattle of what might have been an overturned chair, and the slam of booted feet. Around front a door slammed back fiercely against the log wall, sending forth reverberations, and Ray, guessing that the riders were not, after all, more of Salter's men, sprinted along the north wall until, dropping low, he could peer around in front and sight running men, scattering across the yard. He sought one particular silhouette, but Mort Salter was not among them.

The farthest man, sighting a dark blur of oncoming riders, lanced a winking red gunshot toward them. As before, the night sparkled with tongues of flame.

Miraculously none of the lead caught Salter's man, but he let off a high yelp and sped wildly for cover.

One man, less fearful, knelt, swiftly throwing up his carbine and drawing down a good bead. Ray pushed up his gun and snapped off a hasty shot. It plowed a furrow of dust less than two feet from the rifleman, who twisted frantically toward the house, then also fled out into the night.

Gunshots came intermittently now from around JM's buildings and the riders broke up, some dismounting, some spurring savagely toward muzzle blasts, nearly all calling hoarse epithets in their anger and eagerness to reach cover or Salter's riders, one or the other.

Ray stood fully upright when the fight was at its hottest and moved pressingly along the front of Mitchell's house. He had not seen Salter and meant to find him now while his gunmen were diverted.

The front door was widely open. Beyond, someone had doused the parlor lights but other lamps burned and a soft, rose-colored glow suffused the living room. He stood off to one side of the door, breathing deeply, trying to imagine where the guns within would be, then sprang cat-footedly through the opening, went flat upon the floor, and rolled rapidly sideways. No shot came. He swung his gun in a sweeping gesture, straining to make out human shapes—and bumped violently into something soft and yielding. Without a thought and acting on purest instinct, he grappled with the silent stranger, swung a wild blow, missed, caught at a shirtfront, then very suddenly let go.

"Grace . . . ?"

"Yes," the girl's husky voice said unevenly, then firmed up. "What do you think you're doing?"

He was mighty thankful for the poor light. "Excuse me. I thought it was Mort."

"He's gone. Who's that out in the yard?"

"Perry, I think. Where is Joe?"

"Somewhere," the girl said, beginning to rise up off the floor. "When the firing started, he put out the lights and we all lay down."

Ray caught her shoulder, stopping the lift of her body. "Don't get up," he ordered. "Stay as you were." She flattened upon the floor again. Stray bullets were smacking into the house front. None had yet come through the door or the windows.

"Hey, Joe! Where are you? It's Ray."

"Over here, confound it," came a testy and muffled reply. "What in tarnation's going on out there?"

"A bunch of riders came from across the meadow. It might be Perry Smith. Anyway, whoever they are, they aren't Salter's friends."

"You hear that?" Mitchell called triumphantly. "You hear that, George?"

"I hear it," a dull booming voice said with what Ray thought was something akin to coolness. "Where is Salter? He's in here with us some place."

"No!" Grace called over the echo of gunshots. "He went out through the back of the house when his men ran out front."

"Hell," Joe Mitchell said with great feeling and clear disgust, something Ray was also thinking but did not say. "Hey, Ray, how come you to show up?"

"You knew I'd be along, Joe."

"*Ummmm*, reckon I did, at that." Mitchell's crowing became more discernible, as though he had moved out from whatever he had been hiding behind. "Hear that, George? I tried to tell you the boy wasn't no. . . ."

"I heard," Fenwick said sharply. "We can argue that out some other time."

Fenwick might have said more but at that moment a slug crashed through a window to the accompaniment of tinkling glass and struck with a whacking sound into the fireplace mantel.

"Keep down," Joe squeaked. There was a sound of hasty scuttling in the direction of his warning. "Blast them idiots . . . wagin' a confounded war right in my front yard!"

Grace reached forward, found Ray's arm, and closed her fingers over it as he prepared to move doorward. "Don't go," she said swiftly. "Stay here." He peered around at her face. The very vague light shone darkly red in her hair, and her expression, tight with anxiety, was frankly concerned. "Please stay. . . ."

He did not know what prompted him to do it, then or afterward, but he faced back, reached out, and brought her close against him, and kissed her squarely on the mouth. For a moment she was passive, taking the brunt of his pressure without resistance or reciprocity, and then she raised both arms, encircled his neck, and drew him closer, returning his ardor with an equal passion and possessiveness. Then, equally as unexpected, she pushed him away.

"Go on," she said unsteadily. "But come back, Ray. . . ."

He did not move at once, not until she turned her face away, then he crept close to the doorway, went flat, and inched beyond the opening with his belly knotted, expecting a shot that did not come.

The battle was dwindling. Over its blasting rattle and in the brief interims between, he heard a horseman, then another, breaking away eastward. Try as he might, however, he sighted no one.

He heard a great shout of exultation from down near the bunkhouse, then Perry Smith's voice bellowing: "Hold it! Hold it, boys! No sense in shootin' one another. They're gone."

He waited until cautious shapes began advancing upon the house, evasively moving and holding forth drawn and ready weapons, then he called the sheriff's name, identifying himself.

"Here!" Smith called back. "Over here, Ray." And to his posse men: "Don't shoot toward the dog-gone house, boys. No more shooting!"

He met the first posse men and exchanged curious glances with them, moving past toward the heavy harshness of the sheriff's voice. When he could make Smith out, there were three men with him, two of whom were grinning from ear to ear and prodding forward another man whose arms were rigidly skyward.

"Recognize him?" Smith asked, as Ray came up.

"No."

"He was one of 'em," a posse man said quickly. "Me 'n' Art got around behind him an' he plumb give up." Other members of Smith's posse came trooping up to glower at the captive. Someone suggested profanely that the captive be strung up then and there. Sheriff Smith fixed the exponent of this idea with a hard look and said nothing.

"Anyone hurt?" Ray asked.

Smith snorted. "Too dark to see who a man was shootin' at except for muzzle flares." He squinted forward. "Did you get Mort?"

"Get him," Ray replied acidly, "I didn't even see him. As soon as the shooting started, he lit out through the back of Joe's house."

"Sounds about right," Smith growled. "What was he trying to do up here?"

"Bait me." Ray had no sooner uttered the words than he remembered Salter's two bound and gagged sentinels and told the sheriff where they were. Smith sent men to seek and bring them forward, then he made a cigarette, lit it, rubbed his eyes, and grunted.

"I'm tired enough to sleep standing up," he told Ray, and started past. "Well, let's talk to Joe."

Ray stopped him with an outflung arm. "Perry," he exclaimed, "we can talk to Joe later! Salter's the important one right now. If we hit the trail, we can probably come close to overtakin' him before he gets back to his ranch."

Sheriff Smith exhaled smoke from his nostrils and screwed up his face into a painful expression. For a moment he continued to regard the younger man in dour silence, and then he said: "Listen, I'm not made of iron. Neither are these fellers with me. We'll rest a mite while we're talkin' to Joe . . . then go after Mort."

"He'll be out of the country, Perry," Ray said with protest. "He'll head for his lawyer at Yuma or over the line into Mexico, if he thinks we've got enough on him."

"Let him head where he wants to, Ray. Dog-gone if I'm going. . . ."

"Let me take some of your men, then."

Smith balanced this in his mind for a moment, then shrugged. "If they'll go . . . go ahead. Take all of 'em if you want to. When I'm through here, I'll meet you over at Salter's. All right?"

Ray moved off without replying. He searched out the posse men who were herding forward three of

Salter's men, including the two he had left tied in the trees, and told them of Sheriff Smith's decision. Only two of the eleven men demurred and these Ray left to help Smith take the prisoners back to Welton. The others he sent after their mounts while he in turn trotted out where his ugly buckskin was drowsing, pulled the animal loose, swung across him, and waited for the posse men to come up. Afterward, he led them north until he struck the driven cattle trail, then southeasterly down through the forested night toward Salter's range.

Behind Ray the posse men spoke softly, intermittently among themselves. They were pleased with the results of the fight in Joe Mitchell's yard and some of them, the bolder or more blustery, Ray did not know which, anticipated an equally triumphant meeting at Salter's ranch. Ray kept his mouth closed; he did not feel as confident as they did. Most of them, he reflected now, knew Mort Salter as a big cowman, a man of substance and wealth and power. They considered him only in this light. They did not recognize, being small men themselves, the menace, the wiliness, and savagery that had enabled Salter to rise above them in a financial way. But Ray did. He knew as surely as he knew anything at all that Morton Salter was a long way from being whipped. That the closer Salter's back was driven to the wall, the more deadly he would become. Five years of living among human wolves of the same variety as Salter had planted this certain knowledge deeply within him.

He thought it was just as well the posse men did not know; he would need every one of them now, and whether they were brave men or simply ignorant ones did not matter. The showdown fight with his enemy was nearing and every gun he had would shortly be needed.

There was really nothing else in him as he rode down the darkness now except the pinched-down concentration on this meeting with the man who had sent him to prison. In fact, until he had kissed Grace Fenwick, this vengeance hunger had overshadowed everything else, had changed his life, had changed his heart and his mind without his even knowing it.

Chapter Fourteen

They came down from the uplands in a tight clutch and would not have halted except for Ray. He drew up, blocking the trail, gazing, slit-eyed, through the gloom, suspecting that Mort Salter would not have passed up so excellent an opportunity to establish an ambuscade, for here, where the forest ran out and ended against flat-thrusting cow country, a rider emerging from the trees would make an excellent target.

"Go on!" a man called impatiently, his voice carrying well beyond the last fringe of forest.

"Shut up!" Ray said curtly. "Maybe you want to get picked off like a sitting duck, but I don't!"

The posse men turned silent, considering Ray, each in his own way thinking about caution, about prudence, and generally concluding to abide by Ray's orders. They waited.

There was nothing actually to make Ray wary except the knowledge he had concerning men like Salter. In fact, it was the very stillness, the long depth of hush ahead that decided him finally to rein westerly and skirt along through tree shadows for nearly two miles before cutting out into the open.

There was a little grumbling but not much. What the posse men failed to comprehend was that it was not really in Ray Kelly to wait, either. He had already waited five years, and, even for a man who had been forced to learn patience, there was an end to waiting. But, too, there was a wily blending between patience and impatience; it was the difference between men of reckless bravado and a man like Ray who never deviated, never slackened or wavered in purpose, and therefore stood the best chance of succeeding.

He led his posse southeasterly in a steady lope. Night coolness pushed against him, strong-scented, and overhead the stars spread a paling ferment across a moonless sky. He was lower now and had a feeling that the entire desert country tipped from north to south, ending, so far as he was concerned at any rate, over the line in Mexico. And he felt weary. There was an ache in his side that added up to numbness. His thoughts felt the weight of each facet of his situation here on Mort Salter's range. The men at his back did not greatly cheer him, either; he could have longed for a tougher crew because he knew how rough Salter's men would be. Southerly was the full flow of open country—Salter's route of escape, if indeed the rustler chieftain decided to run for it, while in the direction he was riding was Mort's ranch itself, his destination.

They had been riding a full hour when the land buckled slightly, throwing its shoulders easterly in a long, wide swale that terminated at the big spring where Salter's home ranch was located. Again the possibility of ambushers came up. This time Ray detached two of the likeliest-looking townsmen and sent them on ahead as scouts. They faded into darkness almost immediately, each riding far out in skirmish style on either side of the posse. It was this tactic that brought home to his men that peril might be close and inclined them toward silence and watchfulness.

Off in the east, a pale but luminous rind of watery light appeared inches above the world's farthest rim. It did not lighten appreciably until they were in sight of Salter's ranch buildings, and then its brightness was little more than watered-down steel-gray. It did, however, background Salter's buildings, showing them darkly squat and roughly functional upon the slumbering land.

Here, Ray sent forward to recall his scouts. When they returned, he detailed them both as horse holders, dismounted his men, and, carbine up and ready, led his band forward afoot.

There was here, too, that peculiar hush, that pregnant stillness permeating everything. He was very conscious of it and halted his men when the buildings were close enough to loom menacingly.

"Lie flat," he ordered.

"Ain't nobody there," a man whispered loudly.

With patience Ray said: "The reason that ranch is so dark is because the men over there know better'n to light a lamp. Every ranch in Arizona has a kitchen and bunkhouse lamp lit by this time o' the morning." He waited for the man to speak again. When he did not, Ray turned to studying the buildings. There were horses in a corral; he could not see them, but he heard their nose blowing and stomping; each sound carried clearly.

The number of men at Salter's ranch troubled Ray. He was not a soldier in any sense, and additionally he disliked the idea of leading his Welton men closer, where the experienced gun hands could cut them down. But what remained uppermost in his mind was the number of men Salter had on ahead, waiting.

He had deliberately scattered that Salter herd near Tanque Wells to strip Salter of the riders it would require to gather the stock again, and he had also taken those two shots at the cowman for the same reason, knowing Salter would detach other riders to patrol the upland trails and the approaches to his home ranch.

At JM, Salter had had with him only six men. If that number was close to what remained of his hired hands, the odds were still greatly in his favor because six *good* men with guns were worth ten Weltonites who were not experienced in gunfighting. There was, he finally concluded, only one way to find out what he was up against. He left the posse with orders to remain where it was until he returned or until the men heard firing on ahead, and then went fluidly forward, blending with the night.

He expected to find hidden assassins as he had at Joe Mitchell's place, but he did not. In fact, he got up into the yard without making a sound or hearing one, either, then dropped flat upon the earth, straining to see.

Here, the stillness was deepest, most menacing; here, also, he knew, there were other men equally as straining as he was. He groped for a pebble, located one, and flung it against a nearby shed. Nothing happened. He threw a second stone, this one landing fully upon the verandah of Salter's home where it rolled with a distinct and cutting echo and came to rest.

From the huge log barn an owl hooted. A second owl answered from Salter's home, and, as Ray was wiggling back the way he had come, a third owl hooted from the bunkhouse. He knew what he had come up to find out; Salter's men were spread out so that they commanded each approach to the ranch yard. It was, he thought as he arose and started back to the posse, a good disposition, but in another way Salter's dispersal was an advantage for Ray.

He found the men from Welton, hunkering together in conversation. They arose to crowd forward around him expectantly. He told them what he suspected and detailed them, all but the horse holders, to take positions around the buildings. His specific instructions were to prevent any of Salter's men from leaving the buildings they were in for any reason, even if they wished to surrender. Then he led them forward as far as the ranch yard's beginning and there pointed out the barn, the bunkhouse, and Salter's residence. It was an unnecessary precaution actually; there was not a man among them who had not at one time or another visited Salter's ranch. Finally he took two men with him, sent the others forward, and with his companions skirted widely around the yard to come down behind Salter's house. When he knew the others would be in place, he threw a large rock against the rear of the house and called out.

"Salter! Come out here! The sheriff wants to talk to you!"

There was a long echo but no reply. Ray's companions inched closer. One of them said: "Fire a slug into the house, that ought to fetch him out if he's goin' to come at all . . . which I mightily doubt."

Ray tried again: "Hey, Salter! You can save some fighting by walking out here."

That time he got a reply, a blisteringly profane and guttural roar of defiance. "Come an' get me, Kelly!" the rustler yelled fiercely. "You jailbird whelp, you! Poke your face out where I can see it!"

Ray's face colored at the string of epithets following Salter's words and he said nothing until the last echo died away. "All right, Salter!" he cried back. "I'll walk out into the middle of your yard and you do the same! All I want is a shoot-out with you anyway. No sense in these other fellers getting shot up." He paused, waited, and, when no answer came back, he added: "I'm waiting, Salter, or are you too yellow to face me?"

A gunshot flamed wickedly from a rear window and both Ray's companions dropped to the ground where they flattened out and grew very still. Ray cocked his carbine and fired from the hip, levered up another cartridge, and moved sideways as he squeezed off the second shot. There came into the dwindling echo a tinkle of shattered window glass and before another shot was fired he called forward again.

"Salter, you made a tomfool move splittin' your men up. Every building is surrounded."

He got back an immediate answer. "Yeah? Well, you try to chouse us out of here, Kelly. You're trespassing and I've already sent for help. Before I'm through, you'll wish you were back in your stinkin' cell at Yuma." Salter's voice grew thin with fury. "This time I'm going to watch you get it, Kelly. This time I'm going to stand there and watch my boys shoot chunks out of you!"

Salter's obvious rancor was drowned out by a sudden and unexpected flurry of gunshots around front of the house. Ray beckoned his companions up off the ground and led them along through the soupy light where they could see across the yard. Winking gun blasts from the barn's interior showed where the fighting was. He tried to get far enough northward to join in by facing the open doorway but the bullets were thick there, and he retreated with his two men as far as the woodshed where he stopped.

Salter's men in the log bunkhouse tried to support their friends in the barn but the angle of their building was wrong for that, and, after firing a few rounds, they contented themselves with alternately calling encouragement to the besieged men in the barn and cursing their attackers savagely.

"We could slip around behind the bunkhouse," one of Ray's men said swiftly, his face alight with excitement. When Ray did not reply, he repeated it and looked frowningly upward. "Hey, you gone deaf or something?" he said at last, shaking Ray's arm for attention.

Ray shook off the man's hand. "Go get your horse," he said sharply to the Weltonite, "and ride back to town. Tell Perry Smith that Salter's sent riders for the rest of his crew, and we're going to be chewed up here unless he can round up more men and get over here in a cloud of dust."

"Huh?" the man said in a rising way, frowning. "How d'you know he's sent for help?"

"Dammit," Ray said, giving the man a quick push. "Do like I told you. Didn't you hear Salter say he'd sent for help?"

"No," the man said frankly and honestly, "I didn't."

"I did," the other Weltonite chimed in. "You better do like Kelly says," he told his friend. "And you'd better make sure Sheriff Smith gets back here soon, too, 'cause the way I calculate it . . . Salter's messengers been gone damn' near long enough to round up the rest of his crew and start back."

The posse man said not another word. He trailed

his carbine, spun about, and began zigzagging widely around Salter's house, his every movement full of grim resolve and urgency.

The remaining Weltonite faced around from watching the messenger fade out in the murky light, his face tightened with anxiety. "Maybe you'd best send another man in case he don't make it," he told Ray.

"He'll make it," came the reply. "You take the back corner of this shed and I'll take the front. Keep up a fire on the main house. Salter'll be sweating bullets to know how the fight's going down at the barn." The man was moving off when Ray caught a foreign sound in the air, an ominously quivering, thundering echo from far off.

"Wait a minute!" he called, and the posse man turned back. "You hear anything aside from the firing?"

The townsman cocked his head, frowned in concentration for a moment, then straightened up with a quizzical look and a head wag. "Not a thing but the shootin'," he said. Ray was looking beyond him toward the west. He said nothing. Suddenly the posse man heard it and sucked in his breath. "I got it," he said breathlessly. "I got it now. Horsemen! A passel of riders comin' on, Mister Kelly!" The man's face, unhealthily gray and seamed-looking in this poor light, pushed up close. "It better be the sheriff," he breathed, hearing with more distinctness the drum-roll beat of many riders hurrying. "Hell, if it ain't Sheriff Smith an' a posse, we're done fer . . . out here in the yard with dawn comin' and all . . . Mister Kelly!"

Ray shot the man a look, saw mounting apprehension, and wished again he might have had a better posse. It was not, he thought now, that townsmen could not or would not fight; it was simply the difference between rough men inured to fear and discomfort and personal peril, and those whose environment had not so inured them.

"Go tell the men over by the barn to meet me behind the bunkhouse."

"What for?" the posse man demanded.

"Because we've got to get inside somewhere. Now go on!"

The Weltonite moved off a few steps, then turned back to call: "You don't reckon that is the sheriff?"

"Dammit," Ray said exasperatedly, "you want to get us all killed with your delaying tactics? No! I don't think it's the sheriff. Now, move! Do like I told you!"

The posse man whirled away, driven onward by Kelly's harshness. Ray waited until he was certain the man was going to fulfill his mission, and then he ducked around the woodshed, running in a crouched-over, erratic fashion toward the bunkhouse.

Chapter Fifteen

There were three men behind the bunkhouse, pressing against the dark wall. Dawn had made no appreciable impression there, and, when Ray hissed, then came around the south end of the little log building, two of the three men grew wire-tight and ready. He called forward his name and joined them. The first question was:

"You hear them riders coming?"

"Yes."

"You reckon it's Perry an' a posse?"

"No. Now, shut up and listen." The posse men shuffled closer, half heeding Ray, half gauging the distance of the audibly riding horsemen.

"I don't believe there are more than three or four men in the bunkhouse. We've got to get under cover."

A townsman interrupted uneasily. "Someone's coming," he whispered, turning toward the barn.

"It's the others," Ray said impatiently. "Listen, now. When everyone's here, we're going around front and burst into the bunkhouse." He paused, waiting for protests that did not come. Heartened by this, he then went on. "Once inside, we can hold off an army until Sheriff Smith gets here."

"Unless our ammunition gives out," a man growled.

Another said in an equally despairing voice: "How's Perry goin' to know we need him?"

"Because I sent him a messenger," Ray replied, straightening off the wall as the balance of the posse materialized out of the watery dawn. "Let's go!"

There was a great depth of silence in Salter's yard. Except for the oncoming riders, dangerously close now but still muffled as they rode in, there was no noise from either the barn or Mort Salter's house.

Ray was bent low, moving along the front of Salter's bunkhouse when from within came the sound of a chair scraping over rough pine flooring. This was followed by a sound they all knew—the quick, hard-shuttling rasp of a loophole being uncovered. Behind Ray a man gasped, stifled it, and went nearly flat. His breathing sounded as loudly to Ray as the crackling of a crown fire in a forest. It was not audible to the man within whose eye was straining at the loophole because of the louder sound of riders. Ray heard the man close the slot and say strongly to his companions in a voice filled with revived hope: "They're comin' boys. I heard 'em plain as day."

With a sudden inspiration Ray straightened up, struck the door hard with his gun butt, and called out in an authoritative way: "Open up in there! This is the sheriff! I said open up! If I got to shoot my way in, you won't live to surrender. I got eight men with me out here and you can hear the rest of the posse coming up!" He struck the door again, harder, and the walls reverberated. "I said open up!"

For a moment there was total silence. Then, from within, two voices rose sharply, briefly, until they were stilled by a third, bleak and bitter voice. The first two voices were unintelligible to Ray but the angry third voice was clear enough.

"Open it, Charley," it commanded. "Damn it, I

said *open it!* I ain't goin' to get killed for Mort Salter or anyone else . . . not against odds like that."

That time the protests were louder. "What're you talkin' about?" One of them argued. "Mort's paying us to. . . ."

"Open it!" the same commanding voice broke out furiously. "Mort ain't payin' enough to get killed or strung up. We ain't done nothin' the law can hold us for . . . yet."

"What about the cattle?"

That time, as Ray lifted his weapon to strike the door a third blow, there was a hard slam of boot steps, the creaking rise of a door bar, and the panel swung inward.

Ray pushed swiftly inside. His men crowded over the threshold to fill the bunkhouse, every gun up and steady, bearing fully upon three big-eyed cowboys. The man who had opened the door squinted at Ray and said a savage curse.

"Sheriff?" he snarled. "You're Kelly . . . that's who you are!"

Ray palmed the deputy's badge and held it forward. "Good enough?" he challenged.

Salter's gunman looked long at the outstretched hand; he appeared to be turning something over in his mind. He finally shot an appraising look at the posse men behind Ray, raised his shoulders, let them fall, and said sullenly: "It's good enough." He tossed his handgun on a table. Left no alternative, the other two Salter men did likewise.

"Tie them," Ray ordered. "One of you gather their ammunition and guns." As his men moved out of their tracks, Ray went to one of the three windows, threw it wide open, and listened. The band of horsemen was sweeping up from behind Salter's barn; they were slowing now, breaking over into a choppy trot, scattering slightly, some recklessly by-passing the barn's rear-wall protection for a view of the yard.

Ray sighted a blur of bulky movement, raised his carbine, and fired. The rider jerked his horse high into the air, whirled, and raced for cover behind the barn. Until Ray fired there were only horse sounds; now men's voices sounded quickly, fiercely, calling back and forth.

From over Ray's shoulder a posse man said: "We can't get no good shootin' toward the barn an' the back wall of this dog-goned bunkhouse ain't got no window. They can slip up on us out there."

Ray turned, pushed past the man, crossed to the other windows, and flung them wide, also. This was to minimize injury from flying glass. He then moved along the wall to a safe spot, made a deliberate ciga-rette, lit it, and gazed at his posse.

The townsmen were obviously uneasy over the quick reversal of a situation they had all ridden into with excessive confidence, but they seemed a long way from panic. Ray thought this might not have been the case if he had not gotten them into the bunk-house; here, they could not desert if they wanted to. It was, he thought, the best situation possible under the circumstances, and regardless of the numbers op-posed to them they were safe at least as long as their ammunition held out.

He was not considering the opposite side of the coin. Mort Salter's hatred was nothing to overlook; his vindictiveness and ruthlessness permitted no compromise, ever. Ray Kelly was not the first man, however, who had let down his guard for a moment and found Mort Salter waiting to spring.

Gunshots erupted from over near the woodshed. A ragged volley also came from Salter's house. Lead slugs struck solidly into the bunkhouse logs. One or two of the posse men winced at these slashing sounds, but others crept to the windows, poked carbines over the sills, and risked harmless but defiant shots. Ray told them to save the ammunition. Someone stoked up the bunkhouse stove and put the coffee pot on to boil. Then a bullet knocked the outer stovepipe off and oily smoke guttered briefly to sting eyes and cause choking sounds from the defenders until dawn air sucked it away out the windows.

Someone, from the vicinity of Salter's house, was firing deliberately at the bunkhouse door with a buffalo gun. Each resounding explosion was a bull-bass, great coughing explosion that easily drowned out the lesser carbine *cracks.* The door was hand hewn of tough fir slab wood and would have withstood conventional lead slugs indefinitely, but Ray soon determined that the gunner firing from somewhere near Salter's house was concentrating his fire upon the hinges and each slug made the door quiver from impact. This kind of a shoot-out, he knew, could end favorably for the posse men only as long as they were not exposed to a foe that he estimated outnumbered them approximately two-to-one, and that held not only firepower superiority but also gun-savvy wisdom. Some way, therefore, he had to silence the man with the buffalo rifle before the door was shot away and the bunkhouse's interior was exposed to Salter's gunmen.

Around him and despite three open windows, the bunkhouse air was becoming difficult to breathe because of acrid black powder smoke. When his men stopped firing to dash tears from burning eyes, he called out: "Keep firing! Don't give them a chance to rush us!"

With ears ringing from the increased firing behind him, Ray went to a front-wall loophole, slid back the shingle, and peered out. Dawn was fully up now; Salter's house stood darkly visible and gun flashes winked at him from various places around the yard. He waited for one particular marksman, and, when the great booming explosion came, he drew back, felt the door on his far right tremble from impact, poked his carbine through the loophole, and sighted. He had the rifleman's location estimated but he needed another sighting to narrow it down.

When the buffalo gun blossomed again, Ray snugged back his trigger, leaned into the recoil, and levered up a second shot and a third. He could not see the rifleman so he bracketed the area he knew the man occupied and was rewarded when the buffalo gun was temporarily silenced. He had not hit Salter's gunman, he knew, but he had forced him to change positions. Each time afterward the big-bored weapon made its telltale plume of red fire Ray was waiting. As he and Salter's gunner dueled, the fight around them swirled into a deafening crescendo of winking tongues of flame and flat vicious explosions.

Ray's posse men took heart from their security and became reckless. One of them was knocked flat by a graze over the right ear and the others, thinking him killed, became careful again, firing swiftly, then dropping away from the windows.

The fight had been in progress less than fifteen minutes when the defenders heard a voice most of them recognized commanding the attackers to hold their fire.

Gradually the echoes faded out over the range, and, as Ray drew back, straightening up, to begin plugging fresh loads into his carbine, Mort Salter's voice knifed into the silence.

"You fellers from Welton! Listen, there's only one man in the bunkhouse I want! Send him out into the yard and you got my word the rest of you can ride off unhurt!"

A flush-faced younger posse man made a cold laugh and called back: "You can have him, Salter. Just come on over here and get him!"

Other posse men grinned and laughed. They smiled broadly at Ray, their faces reflecting both confidence and support. Then Salter's voice came again, softer this time, more ominously menacing.

"You had your joke," the rustler chieftain called. "Now I'll have mine. Want to know what it is, boys?"

No one in the bunkhouse replied. Each face lost its smile in a fading way. There was no misunderstanding Salter's changed tone or his deadly confidence.

"Well," he said when no reply came back, "I'll tell you anyway. That firing wasn't to drive you out. It wasn't even calculated to kill any of you." Another long pause, then: "It was to give my boys time to slip up behind the bunkhouse. You hear me, Kelly? They hauled up some coal oil and pitch wood an' put it against your back wall. They're waiting for my signal now, and then they'll set it afire . . . Kelly? That there bunkhouse is made of pine logs. It's been standin' for a good many years. You understand what I'm gettin' at, Kelly? That bunkhouse'll burn like tinder!"

There was more. Salter's triumphant tone went into the skull of every posse man in the bunkhouse.

They exchanged glances and looked away, out the window where sunrise was nearing, or at the tied prisoners on the floor, or at the boiling coffee pot—but not at Ray Kelly.

Half-heartedly someone called to Salter: "Oh, shut up! You talk too damned much, Mort."

The distant voice sounded amused. "All right, I'll shut up. I'll do better'n that. I'll give you ten minutes to push Kelly out that door. Ten minutes . . . an', if you don't throw him out, you'll be boiled alive."

The foremost of Salter's men raised his head off the floor to shoot a desperate stare at Ray. "He means it," the gunman said sharply. "Kelly, he ain't kidding. He'll burn this house down around your ears."

"You'll fry with us," a Welton man growled.

"No," the captive said swiftly. "Listen, you fellers, Mort only wants Kelly. Throw him out the door."

"So they can shoot him down like a rag doll?" someone said.

"All right," the gunman croaked. "So they shoot him. Listen, ain't no life on earth worth gettin' eight or ten men killed over, is there?" The gunman wiggled along the floor, worked his way up the wall until he was in a sitting position, and grimaced at the watching ring of solemn, smoke-grimed, and tear-stained faces. "Disarm Kelly and force him out into the yard. That's all Mort wants. He said he'd let the rest o' you ride out and he'll keep his word."

A posse man said—"Shut up."—and turned his back upon the prisoner, his face showing strong disgust. The same man gazed at Ray. "There's a loophole in this back wall," he said half-heartedly, thinking the same thing everyone else in the bunkhouse was also thinking—it would not be possible to depress a gun barrel far enough downward to fire at the man they knew was crouching there, awaiting Salter's signal to start the conflagration.

Ray crossed to the back wall and pressed his ear to it. He heard nothing at all, so he rapped upon the logs with his gun butt. Immediately, clearly audible to every man in the room, came back a sardonically played tattoo with an answering gun butt. He bent low, opened the loophole, and peered out. The scent of coal oil arose at once to his nostrils. Salter had not been bluffing, but he had never thought Salter was bluffing anyway. From the corner of his eye he caught movement. The back of a man's neck was visible where he crouched, holding a match in one hand ready to strike it and duck away.

Ray worked his face around the loophole seeking other men. He found none. Behind him a posse man's fingers brushed over his shoulder, and, as he turned, the man said—"Here."—holding forth a steaming cup of jet black coffee. "It's too dang' hot to drink and there's no water in here to cool it with."

Ray took the cup, found it as blistering hot as he had been told, and turned deliberately with every eye in the room on him, and poured it with a quick and unerring aim through the loophole. The posse men did not at once understand what he was doing, but when they heard the wild cry of pain from below the loophole, they grasped his purpose and broke into full-voiced encouragement. One of them hastily secured a second cup and held it out. But Ray, watching the fleeing, writhing figure of Salter's gunman shook his head.

"One's enough," he said, with his face against the inner wall. "I've heard folks say someone ran like a scalded cat but that's the first time I ever saw it done."

Outside in the yard Salter's riders were shouting angrily. There was no time to make out what they were yelling back and forth because almost as soon as the badly scalded man was among them once more the gunfire was resumed, and this time it came from every direction around the bunkhouse, more fiercely than before.

One of the sitting prisoners watched Ray cross to the front wall, bend forward toward a loophole, and thrust his carbine through. His face, dank with sweat, lost its appearance of apprehension. He could not refrain from calling to the closest posse man: "He saved our bacon, that Kelly feller! Mort'd have burnt this bunkhouse down sure as God made green apples."

The posse man might not have heard for all the attention he paid.

Chapter Sixteen

Again the fight raged fiercely and Ray, concentrating on the moving marksman with the buffalo gun, did not know a second casualty lay upon the floor behind him until he turned, moving away from the loophole to reload a second time. Simultaneously he saw the posse man sitting in the middle of the room, groaning and holding a bullet-broken arm, and also felt along his cartridge belt to discover that he had no more carbine shells and only half a loop of handgun bullets.

He motioned for a man standing nearby to bind the injured Weltonite's arm, then went to the table, picked up a shell belt lying there that had been taken from one of the prisoners—and discovered that someone had been there before him, the belt hung limply in his hand, every loop emptied of cartridges.

He put his carbine aside, drew his handgun, and tried to estimate the length of time they had been in the bunkhouse so that he could figure ahead to the time Perry Smith would arrive with a posse. Time, passing too erratically, could not be telescoped with any degree of accuracy; he thought they had been in the bunkhouse perhaps two hours. He then revised this downward to one hour, and his heart sank as he sighted the distant horizon from his loophole. The sun beginning to show distantly was not even fully up yet.

They had not been fighting for their lives for more than half an hour, perhaps three quarters of an hour. What chilled him along with this knowledge was the fact that a guarded appraisal of the shell belts around him worn by his companions showed that many were completely empty and none had more than a handful of bullets left in them.

It would, he knew, take Perry Smith a good, long hour to round up a posse and ride to Salter's ranch. He knew also, now, that Smith was going to arrive too late. As soon as the posse's firing dwindled, Salter would launch an all out attack. As he rammed his six-gun barrel through the loophole, he began considering ways of escape, but clearly there was no way out. They were not only surrounded and outnumbered, but now even the brightening new day was against them.

There was, of course, the choice Salter had offered. He was thinking about this when the buffalo gun erupted again. For the first time since the duel had begun he did not answer the shot, but moved tiredly back, closed the loophole, and looked at his filthy, dogged companions.

He thought it was unlikely Salter would massacre the posse men. Even as vicious a killer as Mort Salter would realize he could never escape the consequences of such an act. He would therefore permit the Welton men to ride off unharmed, but Ray's fate had never been in the slightest doubt. Salter meant to kill him and would certainly do it. Further, Salter would do it as he had promised, by shooting chunks off him, killing him slowly, a little at a time.

"Hold it!" he called into the din. "Hold your fire!"

It took a moment for the shout to bring results, but gradually his men turned, moving clear of the windows and looking half quizzically, half hopefully at him.

"We're not going to be able to hold out until Smith gets here," he told them. "There's a way. . . ."

"Sure we will," a posse man stated emphatically. "He'll be along any minute now."

"Look at your belts," Ray said shortly, and watched as groping hands went low to feel along the empty loops, as men's faces changed expression when they gazed at the belts of other men.

"I'll go out," he continued quietly, nodding toward the propped-up captive on the back wall who was watching him through slitted eyes. "Like our friend here said . . . Salter wants me. He won't bother the rest of you."

An angry-eyed townsman said loudly: "No! We ain't got time now for heroics, Kelly. We come into this together and. . . ."

"Heroics, hell," Ray shot back irritably. "Like our prisoner said, no one life is worth a half dozen lives, and, if we wait until we're all killed . . . who'll be around afterward to make sure Salter pays for this?"

There was a short interval of silence. Far back, near the rear wall, a posse man's brow clouded briefly. This man bent, pressed his ear to the wall, then ducked lower, scrabbled at the loophole cover, yanked it aside, and forced his head sideways to the opening. In a hoarse and unbelieving voice he said: "Horsemen! There's horsemen coming!"

A large, raw-boned man forced his way to the same loophole and strained sideways to hear. He rose up, looking breathlessly at the silent, stone-like figures around him. "It sure as hell is," he said.

Beyond the bunkhouse, Salter's gunmen were still firing, but only sporadically, and, when Ray bent to listen at the loophole, he heard a distant call of alarm raised from well north of the barn. The shout was taken up and passed forward. Salter's gunmen had also heard the hoof thunder and were crying questions back and forth.

Ray drew back so others could listen at the loophole. It would not be Perry Smith; he was certain of that. Then who? Realization came abruptly, warming him.

"Joe!" he exclaimed abruptly. "Joe Mitchell and JM!"

A townsman breathed outwardly a fervent curse and wiped sweat from his face with a soiled sleeve. "I've heard lots of tales about old Joe Mitchell," he said, almost prayerfully, "an' I never cottoned to him, but if he's out there now to help us . . . s'help me no one'll ever dast say nothin' ag'in' him around me ever ag'in."

"Comin' fast," a man at the loophole chortled, straightening up and moving toward the north window. "Hey, lookit there," he intoned from his new position against the bullet-splintered sill. "Mitchell's whole blessed crew!"

Ray went to the window and as recklessly exposed himself as did the other besieged men. It was the finest sight of his lifetime. In that softly delicate new daylight the hard-riding band of horsemen swept steadily onward, boring strongly toward Salter's ranch yard, brandishing carbines, and emitting sharp cowboy yells as they rode.

A scattered burst of gunfire met them when the range was right, but Joe Mitchell, well in the lead, instead of slowing, threw back his head, let off an Indian howl, and spurred the harder.

Salter's yard suddenly came to life with mounted

men breaking from cover and riding thunderously southward into the desert. A few other gunmen, sprinting toward the barn after mounts of their own, wasted no time shooting at the exposed observers in the bunkhouse window, painfully visible and scornfully contemptuous of that fact.

"Look at 'em go," a posse man chortled, pointing with an empty pistol at Salter's fleeing riders.

Ray, struck suddenly with the knowledge that this time Salter, expecting no mercy and indeed unlikely to get it from Mitchell, the man he had worked fiercely to destroy, would be fleeing too. With scarcely a thought that there might still be a gunman or two waiting beyond the door, he unbarred it, flung it back, and sprang out into the yard, handgun bared and swinging. No shots came. He began the race to arrive at Salter's barn before the last horse was taken; there was no time to go after his ugly buckskin.

He was in the barn, seeking a mount when Mitchell's JM crowd swept up, dismounted on the fly, and pelted for cover, seeking targets. An occasional gunshot sounded, more from exuberance Ray thought, than because anyone had more than a fleeting glimpse of a target. Triumphant roars rocketed back and forth as Mitchell's riders scuttled among the buildings. The loudest shouts came when Ray's beleaguered posse men crowded out into the yard and junctured with the JM.

He found an iron-gray stud horse in a stall by himself, evidently overlooked by Salter's escaping riders, and led the snorting beast forward to saddle him. He was cinching up when a deep voice spoke down the barn's alleyway to him.

"Is that you, Kelly?"

Ray turned, stiffening as he straightened. "It's me."

The wide-shouldered shape approached. "It's me," the man said, "George Fenwick." He stopped, looking steadily at Ray. "I owe you an apology."

Ray returned to rigging the stallion. Over his shoulder he said sparsely: "You owe me nothing, Fenwick." He bitted the animal, swept up the reins, and toed into the stirrup. "Tell Joe I'm goin' after Salter." From the saddle he added: "Unless you want to try and stop me. . . ."

Fenwick shook his head. "You've got me wrong, Kelly."

"Yeah? Now tell me you didn't send word to Salter I was at the JM?"

"No," Fenwick replied. "I won't deny that. Only . . . you see . . . the way Salter told me, you were a hireling outlaw, a gunman, and a cow thief. I figured I'd be doin the country a favor by. . . ."

"By getting me bushwhacked, Fenwick?"

"I didn't know that was what Salter had in mind. I give you my word on that, Kelly. He said he'd have you arrested to keep the peace. Those were his exact words." Ray started to rein past. Fenwick reached forth to touch and hold the reins. "Hear me out," he said.

Over the swells of Ray's saddle a black pistol barrel appeared. "Take your hands off those reins, Fenwick!"

JM's foreman released the hold he had and ignored the gun. He nodded understandingly. "All right," he said. "I can't blame you. But if you'd let me give you the whole story. . . ."

"Maybe," Ray said, holstering the gun, shortening the reins, and looking steadily down into Fenwick's face. "Some other time." He nudged the stallion, felt powerful muscles bunch under him, then begin to flow with the beast's movement, and passed out into the yard. As he halted just beyond the barn opening, a horseman spun up, threw out a stiff arm, and in a muffled voice said: "If you're after Mort Salter, he went east, not down into the desert." The arm dropped and the rider leaned slightly. "Come on, I'll show you." With a lunge the rider sped away and Ray, hearing his name called, twisted for a backward look as he followed.

Joe Mitchell was sitting his horse, gesturing. "Give him a lick for me!" the raffish old cowman called. He added something else which sounded like "Perry's south" or something similar to that, then Ray was beyond hearing, following the gracefully riding JM horseman ahead, with enough yellow, glittering, bright new sunlight in his eyes not to be able to recognize his guide until, half an hour later and miles out across the range, the rider slowed, drew off, and let Ray ease up to ride stirrup. Then his mouth fell open and his pinched down squint briefly widened.

"You!" he said. "What are *you* doing here?"

Grace threw back his look of astonishment with an uncompromising stare of her own. "I told my father I was coming along. That after what he'd done, we owed you this much. He said I was right." The girl's moving eyes perceptibly darkened. "You look bone-tired," she said. "I . . . I'm not very good at saying I was wrong, Ray. . . ."

"Wrong? Wrong about what?"

She finally dropped her gaze before his stare. "The things you told me about Salter and Joe . . . and about my father . . . they were all true."

Discomfort swept over him. "Never mind that," he said quickly. "If you really saw Salter, just point out the way."

"I'll do better than that, I'll show you," she replied, leaning in the saddle again, booting her mount out in a spurt of speed that leveled off into a mile-eating lope, all her softness, her femininity gone, and her profiled expression showing strong resolution.

Neither of them looked directly at the other again but both, from time to time, stole sidelong glances.

Around them daylight brightened the world. Hours later the same sunlight would be a hard and flinty, faded yellow malignancy, but for that first hour it blanketed the world with promise, with strength, and with an understanding that filled them both. For Grace Fenwick it would be a time long remembered and cherished in her secret heart. For Ray it was a space of time divorced from everything that had gone before; it could have lasted on into eternity and he would have murmured no objections.

Chapter Seventeen

Mort Salter's trail went easterly over the range until Ray considered the likelihood of losing him in the broken country that grew continually rougher as they penetrated it. Then it swung unexpectedly south, held to that direction for several miles, and cut easterly in a purposeful manner that puzzled the pursuers.

"He'll come out somewhere below Welton," Ray told Grace. "I don't understand what he's thinking."

She agreed. "We probably would have lost him in the badlands if he'd continued on eastward."

Ray rode with unconscious effort, concentrating on Salter. The only answer he could arrive at was that the fleeing man was riding now for Welton in the hope that he could buy some guns there who would either stop Ray with bullets or at least delay him until Salter could get a good long start for the border.

The more he thought of this the more reasonable it became to him. It did not occur to him that Salter might have a second reason for riding to Welton until they had progressed along his trail for another hour, then he said: "Grace, he's taking a long chance . . . a calculated risk."

"Oh?" she said, turning a soft and questioning gaze sideways. "Because he knows Perry Smith isn't in Welton?"

"That's part of it. There are two other parts. Mort's

range boss is in jail. If he can get Duncan out, he probably figures Dunc will sidetrack me long enough for Mort to make a clean getaway. The third reason is pretty elemental. Mort's got a lot of money at the Welton bank. . . ."

She nodded slow agreement and for a while said nothing. Then, with Welton showing low upon the sparkling plain, she broke the silence. "I think he would have probably made it if he'd ridden straight for Welton instead of wasting time going east like he did, then having to cut so far south into the desert to get around to his ranch."

Ray was thinking past this phase; his next words proved it. "Joe called out something as we were riding off. I think he said Perry was south of Salter's place somewhere."

"On the desert?" she asked, casting about for signs of other horsemen. "I see no sign of him, Ray."

"He wouldn't still be down here."

They were within sight of Welton now. He drew down to a fast walk, turning gradually cautious. When they were coming onto the village from the rear of its scattered buildings, he told her to split off, to ride to the livery stable, and await him there.

She did not at once comply but neither did she offer argument. His expression was a deterrent; it was a solid-set look that showed clearly that everything but the uppermost thought in his mind was closed out. She slowly drew back, cut obediently across his trail rearward, and angled northerly to enter town from the northerly roadway. The pleasant time when they had been a team was past now; he went to his long-delayed rendezvous with destiny; she went to a lonely place to wait for him.

Welton lay somnolently under the sun smash.

Heat waves danced along the roadway and shimmered from windowpanes. Ray left his horse tied in a dilapidated old barn at the southerly terminus of Welton, crossed to the west side of the road, and started northward to Perry Smith's jailhouse along a refuse-littered and strong-smelling alleyway. He met no one. In fact, the closer he got to the business section of town, the more it became abundantly clear that Welton's citizens were deliberately keeping indoors. This served as a warning but it also served as a means for convincing him that he had, indeed, surmised Mort Salter's destination and purpose correctly. Mort was somewhere in Welton. He thought it a strong possibility that Mort would free Duncan Holt first, and then go for his money at the bank.

He was wrong.

He approached the jailhouse carefully, moving along the adobe wall soundlessly as far as the doorway. Around him the silence and stillness were almost tangible. Behind him, across the alley, were two old wooden buildings. One, which housed the sheriff's horse, showed unmistakable signs of being used, but the second, southerly building, windowless, doorless, and with an old-fashioned outside stairway to its upper story, was very patently abandoned.

No sound came from Perry Smith's office. There would be someone in there, he knew. Smith would not go off and leave Duncan Holt and Carter Wilson unguarded. He considered the possibility that Salter had already been there, had perhaps overpowered the guard. One thing was certain. Welton, as quiet as it was, had been given some recent reason to be so.

He drew off the wall and started past. Where Smith's office and the saddle shop next to it came close to juncturing, there existed a narrow dogtrot, leading fully the length of both buildings from the alleyway to the main thoroughfare out front. He squeezed along this as far as he dared, and paused in the cool murk at the easterly extremity to make a long study of windows, doorways, and the roadway beyond. He caught no reflected sunlight of a gun barrel or any sign of life at all, and stepped into full view, cut swiftly to his right, and flung into the sheriff's office. From across the room Duncan Holt looked up quickly, took in the drawn gun, the sprung knees, and stone-set expression, and slowly stood up to stare.

"Mort been in here?" Ray asked.

Holt shook his head, questions forming and multiplying in his eyes. "No. Why? Is he coming? What happened?"

Ray eased the door closed behind him and leaned upon it, looking from Holt to Wilson. "He got his crew shot up at the ranch and he's here in town somewhere. That's what's happened, Dunc."

From Carter Wilson came a long, wavering sigh. It sounded to Ray as though the cowboy was letting out his breath in relief. Wilson looked through the strap-steel bars at Holt. "It turned out right," he said, the relief more apparent when he spoke. "You figured right, Dunc."

Duncan continued to gaze out at Ray, ignoring the words of his fellow prisoner. Ray leathered his handgun and frowned. "What's he talking about?" he demanded of Holt.

"I told Perry the whole story."

"What whole story?"

"About the rustled cattle, how Mort got rid of them over the line in Mexico, how he's been whittling down the mountain cowmen for years and blaming it on the plains ranchers, then rustlin' from the plains outfits and blaming it on the mountain people so both got to hating each other while Mort cleaned up."

Ray's gaze cleared a little. "You were takin' a long chance," he told Holt. "How'd you know Salter wouldn't find out and have you salted down for saying that?"

Holt made a small smile that didn't come off very well. "I didn't know," he replied, and leaned carelessly upon the bars. "I guess I just got religion, Ray." The crooked smile lingered. "A man sometimes gets off on the wrong foot. . . ."

"And?"

"Well, I been thinkin' in this damned cell. When you're on the owlhoot trail, if you don't get off before it's too late, you're a goner." Holt's smile died out. He fished for his tobacco sack, looking away from Ray's gaze. "What the hell," he muttered. "If you could take five years of Yuma Prison, I reckon I can take it, too." He lit up, blew out a great cloud of smoke, and turned his back, crossed to the bunk, and sank down. "I took the chance. Ray, I got to get off this owlhoot trail before it's too late. When you make that decision, you got to take some chances."

Ray watched his former friend a moment, then drew up off the wall. "Dunc, Salter doesn't know yet what you've done. He hasn't run across Perry yet, and you'd better pray he doesn't, too, because as his foreman you're the one man who can put Mort in prison for a lot longer than five years and he'd do anything to get a witness like you killed."

Holt turned a speculative look on Kelly. "That's up to you," he stated. "If Mort's in town, you're here to kill him. If you get him before he finds out and comes for me, I'll be around in five years or so to hit you up for a job. If you don't get him. . . ." Holt's shoulders rose and fell. He held up his cigarette, examined its tip meticulously, and blew off some gray ash.

Ray turned away, opened the door a crack, peered out, saw nothing at first and was in the act of closing the door again with the intention of awaiting Salter's arrival at Smith's office when from northward up the deserted roadway came a sharp cry of warning. He recognized the voice immediately as belonging to Grace Fenwick. He knew she was sounding an alarm for his private benefit and waited, his gaze raking up along the empty roadway. There was nothing moving anywhere.

From across the room Holt called quickly, softly: "Watch him, kid! He's not fast with his gun but he's as slippery as an eel."

Beyond the oaken door was a deepening hush. Salter knew now Ray was in Welton, he was waiting, too, and, as Duncan Holt had said, he was not just dangerous, he was as wily and deadly as a rattler.

He would not now come to the sheriff's office and Ray knew he had made a mistake in thinking earlier that Mort would think first of his two incarcerated men and secondly of his banked money. It had been the other way around.

He eased the door open sufficiently to squeeze past, drew back a big breath, and sprang through, lit hard on the plank walk, and streaked for the dogtrot. No slamming gunshot came. He paused briefly, feeling sweat running in rivulets under his clothing, then inched his way down the narrow opening toward the alleyway. It was his thought to go north behind Welton as far as the livery stable, find Grace, and determine her reason for calling a warning. It never occurred to him that a man of Mort Salter's stripe would do anything other than lie low and wait for his target to move into view. Ray was concentrating too strongly on offensive action himself to think Salter's reaction might be to free his foreman in order to have Holt's gun as his ally, but as he neared the end of the dogtrot, was in fact pushing forward a long stride to move into the open, a gunshot burst the stillness apart with echoing reverberations and a six-inch splinter of wood was wrenched off the wall on his left. He sucked backward instantly, nearly lost his footing, and threw out an arm to regain his balance. The shot, he determined by a dirty, drifting little puff of smoke, had come from the abandoned old building south of Perry Smith's horse shed.

It required a moment of thought to adjust to this unexpected tactic of Salter's, but he understood it at least. Salter was seeking desperately to free the man he still thought could hold Ray off while he escaped. It was ironic.

Pushing his six-gun quickly into view, he slammed off a wild, unaimed shot at the slatternly old building beyond whose walls, somewhere, Morton Salter was watching. There came a sound of tearing wood, then the rapid reply in kind from Salter's gun. Ray knew what he wished to determine. He drew back a little, methodically punched out two spent casings, flicked the cylinder so that a fresh load lay under the hammer, and gave an abruptly wild jump that left him momentarily exposed in the alleyway, then he sprinted forward, a blur of crouching movement six feet ahead of Salter's third shot.

He made it to a doorless opening in the abandoned building, backed away from the edge of the place, retreating into deeper protection as far as a gaping window casing, and risked a look into the shadowed, cool, and refuse-littered first floor.

The place had been a hotel once, before Welton had grown up in front of it, and the musty, dry odors that lingered there were strong with a kind of discernible nostalgia of the people and events that had once inhabited it. Rats in the walls, disturbed by Salter's shots from within that had set up a reverberation through rotting wood, scurried now with a faint and gritty sound, but this was the only thing for Ray to hear as he moved along the wall to the outer stairway and put forth a booted foot to test the steps. The first five upward-leading shorings were warped but solid still. The sixth one creaked ominously, making a sound that seemed as loud to Ray as if the step had actually broken under his weight, each echo swelling large in the hush. He stepped over it and paused, watching upward and ahead, acutely conscious of the fact that, if Salter appeared now at the head of the stairway, he would be exposed to his fire. A coolness brushed along the back of his neck, an intuitive warning. He moved onward, reached the overhead doorway, and slipped past. Here, with the rotting roof directly above, heat was more solidly noticeable than upon the ground floor. Here, too, there was an odor of disturbed dust and despite the gloom he could make out boot tracks.

He started along the hallway, placing each foot carefully down before moving the other one forward through muffling powder-fine dust. Salter's tracks were his guide, still faint in this hot, deathly still and silent world of deep gloom and deeper hush.

At the first doorway he halted a long time, unwilling to move past without making certain Salter was not crouching beyond waiting to sight movement. Then he stepped wide, cleared this doorless opening—and his foot struck solidly against a broken plank lying athwart the hallway. Instantly a voice came out of the dark shadows to turn him wary.

"Kelly . . . ?"

Ray waited, gun coming to bear in the direction of the voice, keeping silent and watchful as the voice came a second time.

"Kelly? I'm waiting. I've got the hallway covered. I'll give you a chance for your life. Turn around and go back down from here." When no other sounds came beyond the front room where Salter stood, he called more loudly: "You hear me, Kelly?"

"Come out," Ray answered.

"I'll kill you, Kelly," Salter said in a rising tone, and swore.

"Come out, Salter."

Salter's knifing tone came again, more shrill and desperate-sounding now, and the building's emptiness diffused it, making the sound seem to emanate from a dozen different directions at once. Ray cut across it with a third call for the hidden man to come forth. Salter went suddenly quiet and every echo died out to let the deep, formless, and dripping hush return. Ray took a short step across the plank and the floor beyond groaned under his weight. Again Salter's voice came straight down to him.

"You're an outlaw, Kelly. You've been in prison. Anyone can kill you."

"Come on out, Salter."

"I'll hire a dozen of the best guns in the country. They'll track you to hell and back and kill you. I'll pay five thousand dollars to have it done, Kelly, unless you back out of here."

"I'm coming in after you, Salter."

Ray bent, groped behind him for the plank, and deliberately dragged it across the floor, setting up a rough, grating sound of heavy movement. He stopped, crouched forward, and, listening, heard a man's body move ahead of him in a room off his left side.

"Better come out," he said. "I got you located, Mort."

"Five thousand dollars for you dead, Kelly."

Salter's words fell out, hurried and breathless; he could be heard backing away, dragging his feet through dust and litter.

"Kelly? All right . . . I'll give *you* the five thousand. That figures out to a thousand dollars a year for your term at Yuma."

"Not enough," Ray answered, stepping lightly to the corridor's edge where wall joists and flooring merged to form solidness, inching along again to stop just short of the opening into Salter's room.

"Ten thousand, Kelly."

"Still not enough."

"For five damned years? You're crazy, that's more'n you'd make cowboying in twenty years."

"It's not the five years, Salter . . . it's what you just said . . . it's the felon's stain. It's for carrying the memory of being railroaded and turned into an ex-convict for the rest of my life. Ten thousand dollars doesn't begin to equal that out, Salter."

"All right, twenty thousand cash, but that's my last. . . ."

"Come out, Salter."

"Didn't you hear me? I said twenty thousand."

"Will that buy back Joe Mitchell's herd and the other herds? Will it pay for the years of making mountain and desert cowmen hate each other? Will it fetch back the men killed in shoot-outs you engineered, Salter?"

The cornered man shifted position again. Ray heard and brought his gun to bear. He knew how thin and flimsy the walls were and squeezed off a shot. It was a deafening sound that shook the old building. Instantly, over the cracking sound of broken boards, came back a fierce crimson lash of muzzle blast visible in a reflected way past the doorless opening. Ray knew what he had to find out and slammed another shot through the wall, shuttled fully into the framed opening, and let off his final shot before Salter was ready to return the earlier blast.

The last bullet in his gun was the one he had waited five years to fire; beyond the shadowy darkness came a guttering slow beat of failing breath. He holstered the useless gun without moving from that limning doorway, waiting coldly for Salter's last rattle. When it came, he went heavily forward, feeling of a sudden none of the anticipated elation, none of the deep satisfaction he had anticipated feeling for five years, toed the body over, and stood there, gazing downward. He continued to wait for bitter pleasure to arrive, and, when it never did, he made his way out of the building, back down the stairway, out through the dogtrot, and into the lurid sunlight of Welton's solitary broad roadway, empty still. He crossed to a saloon, entered, and crossed to the bar to stand there, exchanging a long stare with the barkeep.

"Sour mash . . . two of 'em."

He was downing the last drink when horsemen beat up into Welton from the south. The barman threw a nervous glance from Ray to the window. He said nothing.

"Another one," Ray said emptily, and, when it came, he tossed it off after the other two as an unhealthy flush began to color his face, to bring a luster to his sight that did not alleviate the emptiness lying there.

"You ate lately?" the barman ventured.

"No," Ray answered. "Set it up, mister."

He was holding the fourth one when Perry Smith and Joe Mitchell burst past the doors, setting them to quivering on their spindles, followed by a horde of sweaty posse men. Sheriff Smith's full glance touched the barman's anxious look, flicked over Ray, and came to rest finally on his face. He crossed to lean upon the bar and speak to the barman without looking away from Ray.

"Beer all around," he said, then: "Some of the boys are takin' him down to the undertaker's shed," meaning of course the body of dead Mort Salter. He drew in a big breath and let it out in slow pinches. "Kid, you satisfied now?"

Ray looked long at Perry Smith without speaking.

"I could've told you," the sheriff went on. "It's one thing to think about killin' a man and another thing to do it." He removed his hat, struck it upon his leg, setting free several layers of dust. "You don't feel good afterward, you feel sort of sick."

Ray faced the barman. "Another one," he growled, and, when the barman looked at Perry Smith, the sheriff nodded without speaking. Beyond him, old Joe Mitchell was standing on Ray's far side, twisting his beer glass in its damp circlet, ruminating. When Ray dashed water from his eyes after the fifth sour mash, Mitchell said: "Kid, I need a foreman. A real good foreman."

"You got Fenwick," Ray said, beginning to hear a roaring.

"Naw, he ain't the mountain ranch type of foreman." Joe turned slightly sideways, pushing his beer glass along the counter. "I need you. Mort danged near busted me, kid. Five years ain't a long time to a feller your age, but it's like a lead weight on a man's shoulders when he gets along about my age. I got to have someone like you who knows the wherefore of our kind of ranchin', Ray, so we can build JM up again."

"I guess so," Ray murmured, twisting to face away from the bar. "I'll be up to see you, Joe."

"No hurry, take your time," Joe said gently. "By the way, Perry's got five confessions. He scooped up about half o' Mort's gun hands heading toward Mexico."

Ray looked toward Sheriff Smith. The lawman nodded but brushed these details aside. His weathered face was carefully inscrutable; he was thinking what Ray would one day discover for himself—that it hadn't been necessary to kill Mort Salter at all. What he said was: "Before that stuff you been drinkin' hits you, Ray, you'd better go down to the office. Grace's waitin' there for you."

"Yeah," Ray said, pushing off the bar.

They watched him leave the saloon in silence. When the doors shivered closed to cut him from sight, Perry Smith leaned fully forward upon the bar and said to Joe Mitchell: "A feller learns a lot in prison, you know, Joe, but where he really gets his education is outside it."

"He'll be all right," intoned Mitchell, faintly smiling.

"Yeah. He'll be all right."

Joe raised his glass. "Grace'll see to that. Drink up, Perry. Five years is a long time to wait for something good to happen around this dog-goned country."

Smith tiredly extended his arm. They drank in silence, gazing confidently and wearily at each other over the glass rims.

About the Author

Lauran Paine who, under his own name and various pseudonyms has written over 1,000 books, was born in Duluth, Minnesota. His family moved to California when he was at a young age and his apprenticeship as a Western writer came about through the years he spent in the livestock trade, rodeos, and even motion pictures where he served as an extra because of his expert horsemanship in several films starring movie cowboy Johnny Mack Brown. In the late 1930s, Paine trapped wild horses in northern Arizona and even, for a time, worked as a professional farrier. Paine came to know the Old West through the eyes of many who had been born in the previous century, and he learned that Western life had been very different from the way it was portrayed on the screen. "I knew men who had killed other men," he later recalled. "But they were the exceptions. Prior to and during the Depression, people were just too busy eking out an existence to indulge in Saturday-night brawls." He served in the U.S. Navy in the Second World War and began writing for Western pulp magazines following his discharge. It is interesting to note that all of his earliest novels (written under his own name and the pseudonym Mark Carrel) were published in the British market and he soon had as strong a following in that country as in the United States. Paine's Western fiction is characterized by strong plots, authenticity, an apparently effortless ability to construct situation and character, and a preference for building his stories upon a solid foundation of historical fact. *Adobe Empire* (1956), one of his best novels, is a fictionalized account of the last twenty years in the life of trader William Bent and, in an off-trail way, has a melancholy, bittersweet texture that is not easily forgotten. In later novels like *The White Bird* and *Cache Cañon*, he showed that the special magic and power of his stories and characters had only matured along with his basic themes of changing times, changing attitudes, learning from experience, respecting Nature, and the yearning for a simpler, more moderate way of life.

☐ **YES!**

Sign me up for the Leisure Western Book Club and send my FREE BOOKS! If I choose to stay in the club, I will pay only $14.00* each month, a savings of $9.96!

NAME: _____

ADDRESS: _____

TELEPHONE: _____

EMAIL: _____

☐ I want to pay by credit card.

☐ **VISA**   ☐ **MasterCard**   ☐ **DISCOVER**

ACCOUNT #: _____

EXPIRATION DATE: _____

SIGNATURE: _____

Mail this page along with $2.00 shipping and handling to:
Leisure Western Book Club
PO Box 6640
Wayne, PA 19087
Or fax (must include credit card information) to:
610-995-9274
You can also sign up online at **www.dorchesterpub.com**.
*Plus $2.00 for shipping. Offer open to residents of the U.S. and Canada only.
Canadian residents please call 1-800-481-9191 for pricing information.
If under 18, a parent or guardian must sign. Terms, prices and conditions subject to change. Subscription subject to acceptance. Dorchester Publishing reserves the right to reject any order or cancel any subscription.

GET 4 FREE BOOKS!

You can have the best Westerns delivered to your door for less than what you'd pay in a bookstore or online. Sign up for one of our book clubs today, and we'll send you 4 FREE* BOOKS, worth $23.96, just for trying it out...with no obligation to buy, ever!

Authors include classic writers such as
LOUIS L'AMOUR, MAX BRAND, ZANE GREY
and more; plus new authors such as
**COTTON SMITH, JOHNNY D. BOGGS,
DAVID THOMPSON** and others.

As a book club member you also receive the following special benefits:
- **30% off all orders!**
- **Exclusive access to special discounts!**
- **Convenient home delivery and 10 days to return any books you don't want to keep.**

Visit **www.dorchesterpub.com**
or call
1-800-481-9191

There is no minimum number of books to buy, and you may cancel membership at any time.
*Please include $2.00 for shipping and handling.